This book belongs to:

....

....

....

OXFORD CHILDREN'S MYTHS AND LEGENDS

Stories from England
Stories from Ireland
Stories from Scotland
Stories from Wales

OXFORD CHILDREN'S MYTHS AND LEGENDS

ITA DALY

STORIES FROM
IRELAND

OXFORD
UNIVERSITY PRESS

OXFORD
UNIVERSITY PRESS

Great Clarendon Street, Oxford OX2 6DP
Oxford University Press is a department of the University of Oxford.
It furthers the University's objective of excellence in research, scholarship,
and education by publishing worldwide in

Oxford   New York

Auckland   Cape Town   Dar es Salaam   Hong Kong   Karachi
Kuala Lumpur   Madrid   Melbourne   Mexico City   Nairobi
New Delhi   Shanghai   Taipei   Toronto

With offices in

Argentina   Austria   Brazil   Chile   Czech Republic   France   Greece
Guatemala   Hungary   Italy   Japan   Poland   Portugal   Singapore
South Korea   Switzerland   Thailand   Turkey   Ukraine   Vietnam

Oxford is a registered trade mark of Oxford University Press
in the UK and in certain other countries

First published as *Irish Myths and Legends* 2001
First published in this edition with selected new retellings 2009

British Library Cataloguing in Publication Data

Data available

ISBN: 978-0-19-272861-6

3 5 7 9 10 8 6 4

Printed in China

Paper used in the production of this book is a natural,
recyclable product made from wood grown in sustainable forests.
The manufacturing process conforms to the environmental
regulations of the country of origin.

AUTHOR NOTE

— ❖ —

The oldest stories retold here belong to the Mythological
Cycle. They were copied by monks in the eleventh and twelfth
centuries from earlier manuscripts, and originated as oral tales.

These stories deal with the Tuatha Dé Danann, a race
descended from the goddess Danu and who had many
qualities belonging to the gods. When they were defeated
by the Milesians they lived underground and were
transformed into *Sídhe* or fairies.

The second group of stories belongs to the Ulster Cycle
and are mainly about an Ulster King, Conchubhar Mac Nessa,
and his most famous warrior, Cúchulainn. They are said to
have lived around the time of Christ.

The Fianna Cycle comes three hundred years later and
tells of Fionn Mac Cumhaill and the Fianna.

The remaining stories are from the Cycle of the Kings,
dealing with the High Kings of Ireland.

Many of these stories were told to me as a child by my
mother, who would have learned them from her mother. I
have also consulted many previous collections. Among them
are: Augusta Gregory, *Early Irish Myths & Sagas*, (London,
1904); Douglas Hyde, *A Literary History Of Ireland*, (London,
1899; repr. New York, 1967); Patrick Kennedy, *Legendary Fictions
Of The Irish Celts*, (London, 1866; repr. Detroit, 1968);
P. W. Joyce, *Old Celtic Romances*, (London, 1879; repr. Dublin,
1961); Eileen O'Faolain, *Irish Sagas & Folk Tales*, (London, 1954).

THE AUTHOR

CONTENTS

❖

THE MYTHOLOGICAL CYCLE

KING NUADA AND THE SILVER ARM

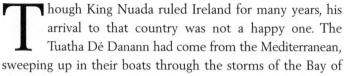

Though King Nuada ruled Ireland for many years, his arrival to that country was not a happy one. The Tuatha Dé Danann had come from the Mediterranean, sweeping up in their boats through the storms of the Bay of Biscay and hoping to find a country where they could settle in some comfort. Things were getting crowded down on the Mediterranean.

When they sighted Ireland, green and misty and inviting, they decided to land there. They sent some scouts ahead, young warriors who swam ashore and scrambled up the rocks to take a look around. When they returned it was to tell their king that the land looked rich, that there was a stream nearby and, most important of all, no signs of any other human beings. So the Tuatha Dé Danann dragged their boats from the water onto a long, white beach, made a bonfire, cooked the fish they had caught earlier, and fell asleep, well content, each one looking forward to tomorrow and their new life.

King Nuada was the first to awake the next morning. He had been given the best place to sleep right beside the fire and now as he turned to warm his back (for the dawn was chilly enough) he opened one eye and let out a most unmajestic scream. For, staring down at him, sitting perched on a high rock was a small, hairy creature, contentedly biting his nails and spitting the bits out in the direction of the king.

'Good morning, your worshipful majesty,' said the small fellow sarcastically. 'And what has brought you to this neck of the woods?'

King Nuada, purple with indignation, hauled himself up as straight as he could before he replied. 'I might ask you the same question, for the last time I saw you and your friends you were heading east. And I was glad to see the end of you and hoping I might never have to look at your miserable faces again.'

For the king had recognized the rascal as a Firbolg—a lowly band of bow-legged bag carriers who used to serve the Tuatha Dé Danann in the old country but who had upped sticks and left one night—every single one of them—to seek their fortune and their freedom in the far east where they had heard that there were countries without kings and where a bag carrier wouldn't be condemned to the life of a servant.

'Ah, we got terrible seasick and the ould boats were blown off course. But—' the little fellow had leapt agilely off the rock and was standing in front of the king, fists raised, '—don't you think you can come here now, lording it over us in our new home. This land belongs to the Firbolgs and you lot can get back into your boats and be off with yourselves.'

With that, he blew a final piece of nail into the king's face, turned round, and was running across the beach and up on the rocks, as fast and sure-footed as a mountain goat.

The rest of the Dé Danann were awake by now and they gathered round Nuada, outraged by what they had heard.

Were they not the Tuatha Dé Danann, the children of the Goddess Danu? How dare a former servant talk to them like that?

'They were always a bad lot those Firbolgs,' said Nuada, 'always looking for wage rises and skiving off when they got the chance.'

An hour later a delegation of five Firbolgs came down to the beach. One of them threw down a long wooden spear in front of the king.

'We give you one hour to get back into your boats and clear out of this place. If you are not gone by then our army will see you off and you will be sorry that you thought to take on the mighty Firbolg. I speak in the name of Sreng our leader and chief.'

The other four threw down their spears then and they all turned and marched back the way they had come.

'It's war then,' said Nuada wearily for he had hoped to leave all that sort of thing behind him. But the young warriors were already rooting around in the boats for their shields and head armour, delighted with the chance of a good fight.

You'd have to feel sorry for the Firbolgs for they were no match for the Tuatha Dé Danann. Smaller and skinnier and less well equipped, their first rank was run through in minutes by the swords and spears of their old masters. By sundown, as many of them lay dead and the white sand had turned red with their blood, they had surrendered.

The Tuatha Dé Danann, being descended from gods, were a noble sort of people and they were generous in victory. They

5

told the Firbolgs that they could start walking away and when they had walked for five days and five nights they could stop and whatever land lay beyond that point would be theirs. (The land the Firbolg occupied was the province we now call Connacht and they lived there very happily for many generations.)

Nuada made this declaration from a litter on which he was carried, for he had been seriously wounded during the battle, his right arm having been cut right off halfway between his shoulder and his elbow. Now as the Firbolgs departed the warriors rushed him into a cave where Diancecht, who was a bone setter and a healer and famous among the Dé Danann for his gifts, began to tie up the stump to stop the bleeding.

This new land was full of herbs and Diancecht, picking them when the dew was still on them, made poultices which he applied to the wound and it began to heal nicely.

'And now I'll make your majesty a silver arm,' he said, 'and you'll be as good as new.'

But that was a lot of nonsense. Firstly, the silver arm had no feeling and was clumsy to use even though it looked well, shined as it was every morning by the king's valet. Secondly, and more seriously, Nuada had to agree to step down from the kingship for there was a rule among the Dé Danann that the body of the king must be free from all blemish.

A man called Bres was appointed regent but nobody liked him and to make matters worse, Nuada, whom everybody loved, seemed to be fading away before their eyes. The flesh of what was left of his arm was hot and swollen and he was in constant pain. And Diancecht had gone off on his travels to search the land for new herbs.

* * *

After three or four years the Dé Danann had spread through-out Ireland (apart from Connacht) and the nobles and king settled in Meath where Bres built a fine palace on the Hill of Tara for himself and Nuada. Though Nuada was still king he had no power and he found the days long and boring and the nights wakeful for it was then that his arm pained him most.

One morning his most loyal servant, Ronan, was up on the battlements keeping watch. Ronan had fought by his master's side at the battle against the Firbolgs and whereas Nuada had lost his arm, Ronan had lost his right eye. Now he stood turning his head, peering with his one eye, when suddenly he saw two young men approaching, riding fine, black horses. They stopped just below Ronan and called out a greeting.

'What do you want?' Ronan was suspicious by nature.

'We've come to see King Nuada. We heard he's not too well,' the dark-haired one said.

'And what business is that of yours?'

'We're the sons of Diancecht and we're healers too and we think we can be of some use to the king.'

'Healers, are you?' Ronan peered down at them with his one eye. 'Then let's see what you can do.' He pointed to his empty eye socket. 'How about magicking me a new eye.' He laughed loudly at his own cleverness. But the two young men didn't seem fazed.

'No problem,' said the dark-haired one. And with that he got off his horse and picked up a tabby cat that had been lying asleep in the sun. He began rubbing the cat and talking to it, then he snapped his fingers together, made a fist with his

7

other hand and, raising it, seemed to throw something at Ronan.

The cat jumped from the young man's arms with a squeal. 'Thief, thief,' he cried and his cat voice sounded hoarse and more like what you might imagine coming from a dog. 'How am I supposed to catch mice now with only one eye?'

'Ah, stop complaining,' the young man said, clicking his fingers again. 'There, you will never get through that feast of mice that I'm giving you now.' And three fat mice appeared in front of the cat's paws. 'As soon as you think you've swallowed the last bite they'll just appear all over again.'

Meanwhile up on the battlements Ronan was leaping around, feeling his new eye and trying it out. 'It's better than my own,' he said. 'Sharper like.'

'Why wouldn't it be? Sure everyone knows that cats see better than humans. Now, will you let us in to see the king?'

It so happened that Diancecht's two sons Miach and Omiach were far better healers than their father and when they saw the king they diagnosed immediately what was wrong.

'The silver is poisoning your system, your majesty, and it will have to come off,' said Miach.

'But how can I go round with an ugly stump where my elbow used to be?' Nuada asked. 'After all, I'm still the king.'

'Leave that to us,' said Omiach, 'for we never half-do a job. Now, look over there.'

And while the king was looking in the other direction Miach yanked off the silver arm. 'That'll make a fine tankard,' he laughed, 'and you'll have a new arm to raise it with before the end of the month.'

The king's wife put him to bed and gave him some mead

to drink to dull the pain while the two young men went back onto the battlements to find Ronan again.

'We want you to take us to the battlefield where the king lost his arm,' Miach said.

'It's two days' ride from here but I'll enjoy finding the spot with the help of my new eye.'

And Ronan found the spot, for the arm had been buried with some ceremony and a small pile of stones still marked the spot where it lay. When they dug down deep they came upon yellow bones, bare of flesh but still in good nick, right down to the finger bones. Carefully they carried what was left of Nuada's arm back to Tara, washing it first in the Boyne River.

'Now, your majesty,' Miach said, 'this will take three days and in those three days you must do as we tell you and remain perfectly still.'

The first day they laid the arm across the king's heart, the second day they laid it across his head, and the third day they placed it carefully against the stump, aligning the bones as best they could. Then they secured the bones with ropes made from rushes, for rushes have great healing powers, and they covered the whole arm, from shoulder to fingertip, with herbs and then covered the herbs in goatskin.

'By Lá Bealtaine your flesh will have grown to cover the bones and you will have a new arm.'

And sure enough, by May Day, when Miach removed the goatskin and the herbs, there was the arm, a bit pink, it's true, and bruised around the joinings but in perfect working order.

Nuada resumed the kingship and Miach and Omiach became his official healers.

The only one among the Tuatha Dé Danann who wasn't completely happy was Ronan, for now, when he tried to sleep at night, the cat's eye was wide open on the look-out for a mouse, but when he was out on the battlements keeping guard and if the sun shone, that same eye would close and poor Ronan, after a sleepless night, would find himself nodding off.

The cat, meanwhile, had grown so fat from the reappearing mice that all the children called him Tiger and gave him a wide berth.

BALOR OF THE EVIL EYE

————— ❖ —————

A very long time ago, many years before Christ was born in Bethlehem, there lived in Ireland a race of people called the Tuatha Dé Danann.

They were descendants of the goddess Danu and because of that they had many gifts of magic. They were also tall and good-looking and they liked poetry and music.

'Give us some sweet music and a sunny bank to lie on and that will make us happy,' they used to tell one another. 'We don't like fighting and war—we leave that to the savage Fomorians. If only they would leave us in peace.'

The Fomorians were a fierce bandit-race that lived to the north of Ireland on a group of islands from which the mists rarely cleared. They were constantly sending raiding parties to Ireland and stealing cattle and snatching children to rear as slaves. They were great sailors and fearless on the sea, and people living along the coasts of Ireland had to keep a close watch on their children for they never knew when the Fomorian boats would sail into sight.

The most savage and merciless king in the history of the Fomorians was a man called Balor. He had only one eye and that eye was so powerful that one glance from it was enough to kill an enemy. As he grew older the eyelid became flabby and he could no longer raise it so he directed that two iron rings be inserted into the eyelid and ropes threaded through these rings. Then when he wanted to kill an enemy he called on his warriors to pull on the ropes and the great, flabby eyelid would be hauled upwards and the eye would turn blearily looking for the enemy. He was known as Balor of the Evil Eye.

Balor never visited Ireland but he sent his soldiers on terrible bloody raids, ordering them to levy a tax on every single person of the Tuatha Dé Danann. 'If anyone refuses to pay the tax, cut off his nose,' Balor said. 'Those Tuatha Dé Danann like to give themselves airs because they are descended from a goddess, but no one can withstand my evil or the power of my eye.'

King Nuada was the ruler of the Tuatha Dé Danann and he knew about Balor and what he could do. 'We'll pay his taxes,' he said, 'and then he might leave us in peace.'

So once a year the king and his nobles waited on the Hill of Uisneach near Tara to give the gold they had collected to Balor's soldiers. 'Better to be safe than sorry,' King Nuada said. 'I don't want to see any of my subjects walking around without a nose and I certainly don't want Balor of the Evil Eye arriving in Ireland. Not even the strongest magic from our druids can do anything about that man—we'll just hope he never decides to come to pay us a visit.'

So one April morning King Nuada and all his nobles were gathered waiting for the tax collectors with a big pot of gold in front of them. Suddenly there came riding across the plain a band of warriors led by a young man whose face and long gold hair shone like the sun. This was Lugh of the Long Arm, famed throughout ten kingdoms for the bravery of his deeds and the power of his magic. Nuada knew about him and that he was the foster son of Manannán Mac Lir, the god of the sea, and that his foster father had given him a special sword that could cut through iron and a boat that could travel over land and sea with equal ease. It was said that he was a good person who never abused his power.

'You are welcome, Lugh,' said Nuada as the young warrior approached. 'It would be an honour for me and my people to entertain you here in Uisneach. Please stay and I will get my servants to prepare a feast for you and your men.'

He was just about to order the great doors to the feasting hall to be thrown open when a shouting and clashing of spears on shields was heard and the Fomorian tax-gatherers came marching over a hill.

Lugh stared at them in disgust. 'What a horrible bunch of people,' he said. 'I don't think I've ever seen a dirtier or uglier gang—who on earth are they?'

As he asked this he turned towards Nuada and was amazed to see the king, white-faced, drop to his knees, as did all of his nobles.

'It's the Fomorians,' Nuada whispered. 'Lugh, please, just do as I'm doing. As long as we show them some respect and I hand over the gold I have collected they will go away and leave us in peace.'

Lugh looked thoughtful. 'The Fomorians,' he said. 'I know a fair amount about those people.'

'You do?' asked the king.

13

'Yes, and you need have no fear, though they *are* a gang of ruffians. I and my warriors will send them off pretty quick, just you wait.'

This was not what King Nuada wanted to hear. 'No— please,' he cried. 'I beg you to do nothing rash. You don't know about Balor and his evil eye, and you don't know what you are bringing down on yourself by attempting to fight against him.'

Lugh gave the king a strange look. Then he laughed. 'I might know a great deal more about that Balor than you imagine, a great deal more than most people do, in fact.'

'What do you mean?' asked King Nuada.

'It's too long a story to start telling you now, but relax and don't be alarmed—I know what I'm doing.'

And with that he drew his sword from its scabbard and waved it over his head. He rushed into the middle of the Fomorians and within minutes most of them lay dead on the ground. Lugh looked at the few cowering creatures that he had spared.

'The only reason you haven't been killed too,' he told them, 'is so that you can go straight back to Balor and tell him that he will get no more gold from Ireland, ever again. And tell him to mind his manners or I'll have to go up there and teach him a lesson myself.'

The nine remaining Fomorians took to their heels, running in a panic back up the hill, not stopping to collect their weapons, much less attempting to take the pot of gold in front of the king. They did not stop, even to draw a breath, until they reached their boats which they had moored off the shores of County Louth. They flung themselves on their oars and made good time back to their northern home, given energy by the terror that filled them. A worse fate awaited them, however. When Balor heard their story he roared for his special henchmen to come and haul up his eyelid. Then he flashed the eye in the direction of the nine tax-gatherers and they fell down dead on the spot, their chests torn open and their hearts pierced by the poison from Balor's eye.

'That is the fate of all cowards,' Balor said. 'Now let us gather all our forces and set out for Ireland so that I can deal with this puppy who has dared to insult me. On the journey I can think of a really painful death for him, something slow and lingering. He will die an inch at a time.' And he laughed a horrible phlegmy laugh.

It took Balor and his army five days to reach Ireland. They moored their boats and began the march to Uisneach with a great stamping of feet and shouting and beating of drums. So great was their number and their power that the earth of Ireland trembled and the noise of their arrival reached King Nuada in his palace. Lugh of the Long Arm also heard the noise. He went at once to the king. 'So,' he said, 'Balor has arrived. I'm really looking forward to this. In fact I've been waiting for such an occasion most of my life.'

The king, who had been eating his breakfast, pushed away his untouched egg. 'I've lost my appetite,' he said. 'I'm not normally a coward but nobody can withstand Balor of the Evil Eye.'

'Nobody except his grandson.' Lugh spoke quietly. 'It has been foretold by the stars that Balor will be destroyed by his own grandson.'

'Much good that'll do us,' the king said gloomily.

The young warrior smiled and came and sat beside the king. 'You know that I was fostered by Manannán Mac Lir?' he began.

'I do indeed.'

'But you have no idea who my blood family is?'

'None,' replied the king. 'And with all due respect, Lugh, I don't think this is the moment to start telling me the story of your life.'

'Then listen to me and you will understand.'

Then he told King Nuada the story of his life. 'My mother was a beautiful young princess named Eithlinn, the only child of King Balor of the Evil Eye—'

He stopped as the Tuatha Dé Danann drew in their breath in surprise and fear.

'The day Eithlinn reached her thirteenth birthday her father locked her away in a tower for he had been told by a druid that he would be killed by his own grandson and he was determined that Eithlinn would be kept forever from the sight of men. This way she would never marry and have children and so his safety would be guaranteed—or so he thought. But one day a great warrior from this country was shipwrecked off the coast of the island where Eithlinn was imprisoned. Cian—for that was the name of the warrior—Cian swam ashore and was thinking that he might have to spend the night in a cave which he had found. Suddenly he heard sweet singing coming from above his head. He climbed upwards and eventually came out in the lower room of the tower where Eithlinn was imprisoned—he had found a secret entrance that nobody knew about, made by pirates a hundred years before.

'Continuing to follow the sound of singing he quickly arrived in Eithlinn's bower and there the young man looked at the young woman and no sooner looked but they immediately fell in love.'

There was a sigh of pleasure from those sitting listening to Lugh's story.

'I love a good romance,' said King Nuada.

'They were together for only a short time because Cian had to return to Ireland. When he had gone Eithlinn found that she was expecting a baby and eventually she gave birth to a son. When Balor heard this he shook with fear and rage. He tore the baby from Eithlinn's arms and took it straight down to the kitchens. "You," he said, calling to a servant. "Take this horrid brat and put it in that basket and fling it into the sea. Everyone is trying to defy me, even my own daughter, but they'll all find that Balor will not be destroyed by any prophecy of the stars."

'The servant was not such a monster as his master and he made a little raft and tied the basket to the raft and set the raft adrift on the sea, making sure that it was out far enough to be clear of any rocks. Some three days later that baby was found by Manannán Mac Lir, and that baby was me, of course. Manannán reared me as his foster child, though since then I have been re-united with my blood father.'

King Nuada was amazed. 'What a story,' he said.

Lugh smiled at King Nuada. 'You see why I laughed when I heard who was at the head of that band of ruffians. I, of all men, need have no fear of Balor. And though he is my grandfather, he is an evil man and I will fight on your behalf, for I know that you are a just king and that these people, the Tuatha Dé Danann, have suffered enough over the years at

17

the hands of the Fomorians. And after all, they are my people too on my father's side. I am half Tuatha Dé Danann through the blood of Cian.'

The morning of the battle was clear and sunny and too hot for the Fomorians who lived in such a cold place.

Under the shadow of the Hill of Tara the two armies were drawn up in battle formation. King Nuada looked with pride at his soldiers and thought that if bravery won the day then the people of Ireland need have no fear. He inspected his troops, then took his place at their head.

Balor, however, sat down on a great rock, his eyelid lowered in case his eye should accidentally fall on one of his own side.

'Let battle commence,' the cry went up and thousands of swords were drawn from their scabbards.

The battle raged back and forth with both sides showing courage and determination. They fought under a hot sun, sweltering inside their armour, and the clanging of swords on shields could be heard as far away as the Giant's Causeway. By noon many bodies lay on the ground and many wounded were being carried off on litters, moaning in pain. But the soldiers of King Nuada fought through love and pride and not through fear and by early afternoon they were advancing on the Fomorians, pushing them back towards the sea.

Then one of Balor's favourite warriors had his head chopped off with one clean cut and the head rolled and rolled until it landed at Balor's feet. Balor gave a great bellow of rage. 'Enough is enough,' he roared. 'Raise my eyelid.'

Ten men ran forward to do his bidding. They threaded the ropes through the iron rings and slowly the lid was raised. 'Now,' Balor bellowed again, 'turn me and direct my eye at that first line of the enemy.'

The men did as they were told and the evil eye was focused on the Tuatha Dé Danann and immediately a hundred men lay dead. The eye flashed again and another hundred fell. Then another. If this continued King Nuada's army would be wiped out.

'Get down, get down,' shouted the king. 'Get down on the ground and save yourselves from Balor's evil eye.'

All around him men fell to the ground until there was only one left standing. Lugh of the Long Arm stood and gazed upwards at his grandfather. He raised his long arm, took aim, and sent his spear flying through the air. So accurate and powerful was his throw that the spear pierced the very pupil of Balor's eye and pushed the eye out through the back of Balor's skull. As it fell the eye lighted on a thousand Fomorians and killed them before it lost its glitter and came to rest on the ground. And as the life ebbed from Balor's body, the light left the evil eye.

With the death of their leader the Fomorians lost their appetite for war and soon they began to retreat. As the sun began to set behind the Hill of Tara the only Fomorians left were the dead ones whose bodies lay strewn on the ground. Nuada sent orders that all his wounded warriors should be brought into the palace where they would be looked after. Over the battlefield hung the stench of blood but most of it was Fomorian blood.

That night some soldiers of the king were out making sure

that no wounded warrior had been overlooked. As they searched they found the huge, evil eye and not knowing what it was they decided to chop it up as food for Nuada's hounds.

Lugh of the Long Arm became a great hero in Ireland where at last there started a long reign of peace and prosperity.

THE CHILDREN OF LIR

— ❖ —

When Lir's wife died he didn't dwell on his own grief but thought only of his four little children and their sudden loss.

What will they do without a mother? he thought. How will they cope? I should try to find myself a new wife so that they will be motherless no longer.

'Fionnuala,' he said, calling his eldest child aside. 'I've decided to get married again for I know well how much you four are missing your mother. All I have to do now is decide who would be suitable to replace her.'

Fionnuala frowned, then shook her head. 'Father, we don't need another mother,' she said. 'I am old enough to look after my little brothers—I can even try to look after you if you'll let me.'

But parents never listen to their children and Lir, always sure that his decisions were the right ones, began to think whom he could marry.

At once his thoughts turned to Aoife who was the younger sister of his dead wife. Would she not be an ideal choice, already the children's aunt, sure to cherish them and love them?

21

Aoife was very beautiful, with skin like cream and hair as dark and shiny as blackberries growing in a sunny hedge. She was also vain, however, and had a jealous nature. When Lir proposed to her all she could think about was the fine life she would lead married to a powerful king, with wealth galore and friends throughout Ireland. She imagined the children being minded by servants while she and Lir enjoyed themselves, throwing parties and going on holidays. And everyone admiring her beauty, dressed as she would be in jewels and silks.

They were married in early spring and already by the end of June Aoife was feeling pretty fed-up with her new life. It seemed to her that the palace had been turned into one big playroom for the children with their toys in every room and the long gallery serving as an indoor sports pitch. Lir never wanted to go anywhere or do anything, just stay at home with what he called 'our happy little family'. If only the children were not there . . .

With this thought, there flashed into Aoife's mind another: why not get rid of them? With the four of them gone she was sure that Lir would begin to pay more attention to her; as he should do considering that she was his wife.

It was a very hot summer and one morning after breakfast she said, 'Dear husband, I think I'll summon the chariot and take the children for a picnic and find a lake somewhere to have a swim. It's far too hot to hang around here all day. What do you think?'

Lir was delighted to see Aoife taking such an interest in the children. 'I think it's a terrific idea,' he said. 'Go and tell the charioteer to choose the fastest horses and the most comfortable chariot—I want you all to enjoy yourselves. And get the cook to pack fresh strawberries and a pint of thick, yellow cream from the dairy. This should be the first of many picnics for our little family. I'll go on the next one myself.'

Aoife sniggered but he didn't hear her.

They set out along the dusty paths which served as roads in Ireland in those days. They travelled for what seemed like hours to the children.

When they finally arrived at the spot which Aoife chose, Fionnuala could glimpse an expanse of shining water through the trees. It looked cool and inviting, particularly as they were feeling so hot and sticky after the journey.

'Please may we go and paddle straight away?' she asked.

'Of course, my dear.' Aoife's laugh was sinister but the children were too excited to notice.

The water was freezing despite the heat of the day. Fionnuala took Fiachra's hand and Conn began to splash Hugh, shouting with delight. Soon they were all soaked.

'Never mind,' Fionnuala said, 'our clothes will dry quickly in the sun.'

Suddenly they heard Aoife call from the shore. 'Attention, you four, turn and look at me,' she called. 'Stand still and look at me.'

They turned and watched as she widened her eyes, seeing in amazement that they were beginning to glow bright red. Then she raised her hands and pointed her fingers at the children. Rays like streaks of lightning shot from her fingertips and landed on the children and as they did, each child felt a prick, like the sting of a nettle. Then strange sensations began to happen in their bodies. Fionnuala felt as if something were yanking her neck, pulling it upwards, making it long. Her shoulders began to itch where feathers started to sprout.

Hugh looked down at his feet, feeling something between his toes—he was growing webs! Fiachra and Conn felt their lips harden and crackle as they were turned into beaks. Within seconds of the magic spell resting on them they had been turned into four beautiful white swans.

Aoife's cruel laugh sounded from the shore. 'This is my spell. For three hundred years you will remain here on Lake Derravaragh. Then you will fly northwards to the Sea of Moyle. After another three hundred years you will travel to Inishglora and there you will stay for a further three hundred years. When you hear the sound of a Christian bell bringing the new religion to this land you will know that the hour of your release is at hand.'

The four children, four swans now, were filled with terror and dismay. Tears welled up in their bird-eyes and spilled over onto their downy breasts, making the feathers sodden and matted.

Seeing their sorrow Aoife felt a momentary pity. 'I will leave you this consolation,' she told them. 'You will retain your human voices so that you can talk and sing to one another.'

When she arrived home she found Lir pacing up and down on the ramparts of the palace. 'Can it be true?' he asked her. 'The charioteer loved my children and he told me a terrible story—'

'Terrible nothing.' Aoife's laugh was brazen. 'They were nothing but spoilt brats. I'm your wife, after all, and now perhaps you can pay me some attention. They'll do fine swimming around there for the next three hundred years.' And she tittered.

Lir was overwhelmed by sudden fury. Taking up a druid's wand he pointed it at her and she was changed into a demon of the air and disappeared in a puff of smoke never to be seen again.

Then Lir set out at once for Lake Derravaragh. When he arrived there and saw the beautiful swans swimming serenely on the water and heard their beautiful sad voices, his heart nearly broke in two. But Fionnuala swam close into the shore and said to him, 'Don't be sad, father dear. Now that you have arrived I don't feel too bad. Now at least we can all live together once again and we can still talk and sing to you.'

And strange to tell, many years passed with much happiness. At night the swans sang beautiful songs and during the day they chatted to their father about the olden days. Lir had moved his household to the shores of the lake and his servants built him a little house so that he might always be within sight of his dear children. A sweet calmness hung over Lake Derravaragh and visitors often came to look at the beautiful swans who could talk and sing with human voices.

However, Lir could not live for as long as three hundred years. Eventually he died and though he was a very old man the swans were sad. Their only consolation was that by craning their long white necks they could glimpse the grave where he had been buried on the edge of the sand.

Then one day Fionnuala said to her brothers, 'Today we must say goodbye to this place, for the time has come for us to fly off to the Sea of Moyle.'

Together they rose into the air, spreading their wings as they flew over the grave of their father.

They flew northwards and as they travelled the sky darkened and the wind rose. Night had fallen by the time they arrived at the Sea of Moyle but they could feel its choppy waters under them and a cold wind blew from the frozen north, cutting through their feathers. It was a truly desolate place where few people ever came, where seagulls and other, bigger birds shrieked overhead day and night, frightening the poor swans and silencing them with their angry caws. At night Fionnuala would take two of her brothers under her wings as she sheltered the third with the feathers of her breast.

Summer was the same as winter and storms raged night and day. The wind never stopped blowing and often the swans were hurled against rocks by its force. Hugh and Conn had their wings broken on more than one occasion and Fiachra had his poor beak smashed. Fionnuala looked after her brothers as well as she could and she was especially good at keeping up their spirits, singing to them softly and always telling them that when the Christian bell sounded their hour of deliverance would be at hand.

Eventually the three hundred years were up and they took flight again. They had to cross the country to the western sea and when they flew over the place where Lir's palace had stood so proudly they saw that nothing now remained and sheep grazed where once Lir had ruled.

Inishglora was a milder place than the Sea of Moyle but the swans' hearts were heavy with loneliness and their songs became sadder with every passing day. Even Fionnuala found it difficult to be cheerful as she could feel herself grow old and stiff and still there was no sound of that bell. They discovered that swans too can develop arthritis and swimming became difficult and bending their long necks in search of food sent pain shooting through their bodies. They looked as beautiful as ever but the children of Lir were growing old.

One afternoon as they were resting, having a little snooze with their heads under their wings, they were awakened by a strange sound. It filled the air around them, sounding out on a single repetitive note. At first they were frightened but then Fionnuala with dawning excitement realized what it was. 'It is the bell, the Christian bell,' she said, 'the one Aoife told us about. Come on, let's swim towards the sound and try to find it.'

They swam to the shore and began to make their way up a narrow path, moving with difficulty for it had been a long time since they had stood on dry land. They followed the sound and it led them to a tiny stone chapel. By the wall of the chapel a man was pulling on a rope and each time he pulled a great iron object high above his head swung upwards. It was the iron tongue of this object, striking against its side, that made the sound. The swans had found their bell.

The man turned to look at the swans, extending a hand towards them. But when Fionnuala spoke he let go of the rope and started to run away in terror.

'Please,' Fionnuala called after him. 'Please wait and hear our story. We are the children of Lir who were turned into swans.'

When the man—he was a monk, a holy hermit living all alone—when he heard their story he was moved to pity for them and he made them a big, soft nest in the shelter of a hawthorn hedge.

'I've heard about you,' he told them. 'When I was a child my mother used to tell me your story and it always made me so sad. How glad I am that you have come here.'

Every day after that he brought them food and sat to listen to the stories they had to tell, stories of ancient Ireland, of a time when spells and magic were practised everywhere. And he told them about his Ireland and about the new religion which had come to the land.

But soon he noticed that the swans were in failing health. Fiachra was finding it hard to breathe and in the mornings Fionnuala had great difficulty in straightening out her neck.

One morning the monk arrived with their breakfast, a mixture of pondweed and herbs which he had discovered they liked. Then as he rounded the bend he stared in amazement at the sight that met his eyes and the basin he was holding fell from his hands.

Lying back against the nest were three ancient little men and a withered old woman. 'Baptize us now, holy man,' croaked the old woman. 'Baptize us now for the hour of our death is at hand.'

They died that night, baptized in the Christian faith. The monk buried them under a giant oak but that was many centuries ago and all traces of their grave have long since disappeared.

Nobody really knows where they are buried but sometimes at dusk children walking along a certain lonely road in the west of Ireland hear singing, beautiful singing which seems to come from the air around their heads. The voices are childish, the songs sung in some ancient tongue.

Tradition in that part of Ireland has it that those childish voices are the voices of the Children of Lir, still singing to us down the ages. I believe in that tradition.

MIDIR AND ETÁIN

❖

The Tuatha Dé Danann lived happily in Ireland until one spring when the seas were calm, the Milesians, journeying from the middle of Europe, invaded the country and a long war ensued.

The Tuatha Dé Danann fought bravely but they were outnumbered and in defeat they retreated to the hills and mountains and built themselves forts and raths underground. There they took up a new existence and became known as the *sídhe* or fairies and the land they lived in was known as the Land of the Ever Young or Tír na nÓg. This was a country where there was no sickness or sorrow or death, a beautiful land of gentle winds and a sun that never burned too hotly but shone its golden light into every home. Sometimes the sídhe came out into the mortal world and sometimes even married a mortal but always, always they remembered Tír na nÓg and they wanted to return to it.

One of the princes of the *sídhe* was called Midir the Proud and he lived in a rath on Callary Hill outside Dublin with his wife, Fuamnach. Out hunting one day he came upon a beautiful girl called Etáin. She was lying in the shade of a rowan tree, making a necklace from the rowan berries that had fallen at her feet. Her lips were as red as the berries, her neck as graceful and white as a swan's. Immediately Midir fell in love with her and getting off his horse he said, 'You are so beautiful, you must marry me and come home with me as my second wife.'

In those days it was quite a common custom to have more than one wife, especially among princes who had plenty of money. However Fuamnach flew into a rage when she saw the beautiful creature she would now have to share her husband and home with.

'I'll not stand for such treatment,' she fumed silently, while all the time pretending to make Etáin welcome. 'I'll soon sort out that pair.'

So she went to a druid to ask him, could he make a spell to get rid of her rival. The druid gave her a little red pill. 'Drop that into a cup of red wine so that the colour will be disguised. And don't worry for it has practically no taste. Make sure that the girl drinks down every drop and then wait for the fun to begin.'

The next day when Midir had gone out to see to his horses, Fuamnach invited Etáin into her part of the palace and there offered her a golden goblet filled with red wine. 'This wine is particularly sweet and delicious,' she said. 'Drink it down and then we can have a nice, cosy chat.'

As soon as Etáin had finished her drink there was a great sound of rushing wind and a black cloud covered the sun in a total eclipse. When light was restored Etáin had disappeared, but fluttering in the air over Fuamnach's head was a lovely butterfly with bright, jewel-like wings. The wings were the same golden colour as Etáin's hair, with delicate markings the same blue as her eyes.

Taking up a broom Fuamnach beat the poor butterfly out of the window, where a terrible storm was brewing, another part of the druid's spell.

For seven years the butterfly was buffeted by the winds up and down the counties of Ireland, never able to rest, often suffering extreme cold, or burning heat when the wind lifted her too close to the sun. Then by chance a gust blew her through one of the windows of a fort near the river Boyne. This was the fort of Aengus and he, being also a *sidhe*, immediately recognized Etáin, disguised though she was as a butterfly. The *sidhe* always recognize one another, no matter what disguise they adopt.

Aengus had not the power to undo the druid's spell but he was able to remove it at night so that from the appearance of the first star in the sky until the sun began to rise the following morning Etáin resumed her shape as a young woman. Aengus fell in love with Etáin and made her a special glass dome where she was protected from the wind during the day. He filled the dome with sweet smelling flowers and shrubs and she gathered nectar from these and so she lived and grew even more beautiful, both as a girl and as a butterfly.

But Fuamnach found out where she was and, still consumed with jealousy, she went back to the druid. 'Do something at once,' she demanded. 'I don't want to hear about that wretched girl having a good life with Aengus. Get her out of there at once.'

So the druid created another storm which sent the glass dome crashing to the ground, caught up the butterfly on its current, and lifted her above the fort on the Boyne and away from Aengus. The poor butterfly, feeling the wind tearing into her fragile wings, knew that another period of suffering was beginning for her.

In all this time Midir never ceased to look for his darling Etáin but, of course, he was looking for a young woman and not for a butterfly.

After another seven years she was blown in through the windows of Etar, a famous Ulster warrior. By this time the butterfly was exhausted. She flapped her limp wings, feeling she could not stay airborne much longer. Then she found a little ledge high up on the wall and though it was too narrow even for a butterfly to rest on she was able to cling to it. Underneath her a feast was taking place, with people gathered round a table drinking wine and listening to the music of a harp. The butterfly clung on, hoping that the people underneath would leave soon, but as she waited her strength gave out and she found herself falling through the air down into a goblet which Etar's wife was just raising to her lips. Not noticing what had happened the woman drank her wine, noting as she did how particularly sweet it tasted. Nine months later she gave birth to a baby girl who was called Etáin, daughter of Etar.

Etáin, born a second time, grew up to be just as beautiful as before. Her parents loved her and she was happy, for all memory of her life in Tír na nÓg had been wiped away and now all she knew was this world of mortals.

When Etáin was eighteen years old the High King of Ireland looked round his palace at Tara and said to himself, 'I am powerful and rich but I am lonely. It's time that I found myself a wife.' So he sent for his courtiers and said to them, 'You see how dreary my life is here. I want you to search throughout the country and find me a suitable wife. She must be beautiful and of noble birth and she must never have had a husband before—these are the only three conditions I lay down for you. It should be easy enough to find such a young woman—after all, I'm the best catch in the country.'

They set out and after three months they returned and described to him the young women they had seen and picked out for him. He listened carefully. 'I think I'll go and have a look at this Etáin,' he said. 'From the description you have given me she seems like the perfect wife for a High King.'

He set out for Etar's palace but before he reached it he came upon a group of young women sitting on a grassy slope. One sat in the middle combing out her hair with a gold and silver comb. The High King noted her grace and when she turned her head and he saw her face he decided that so special was she that she must have been born in the land of the *sidhe* and there and then he decided to make her Queen of Ireland.

He dismounted from his royal steed and approached the girl. 'I am Eochaidh, High King of Ireland,' he said, 'but at this moment I am nothing but a poor suitor begging you to marry me. I have fallen in love with you and will marry no one else.'

The young woman turned to him. 'I am Etáin, daughter of Etar,' she replied. 'I have never fallen in love though many men have courted me. Now I see how much you love me and I will marry you.'

Tara became a very different place with the new queen installed. She loved music and parties and there were always musicians invited to the court and great celebrations held to which friends and subjects were invited.

On the eve of Samhain, or Hallowe'en as we call it, Etáin and Eochaidh held a party to which they invited two hundred guests. Wild boar and whole salmon were prepared for the supper and gallons of mead and wine. The ovens in the palace kitchen had been red-hot for a week and servants had been sent out to gather all the autumn fruits in the hedgerows throughout Ireland. Etáin wore a green and gold dress with a sapphire necklace to match her eyes and ruby rings the colour of her lips—she had never looked so beautiful. She came down to the great hall to welcome the musicians and choose the music with them before the guests arrived. As she was talking to them she saw a beautiful young man with golden hair, wearing a purple cloak, ride up to the palace on a white horse.

A few minutes later he came walking in the door of the great hall. Etáin went to meet him, wondering who he could be for she had never seen him before. Instead of bowing before her, as everyone did to the wife of the High King, this young man threw his arms around her and kissed her on the mouth.

'At last, at last I have found you,' he said. 'Darling Etáin, I have searched for you for years and now you must leave this place and come back with me to Tír na nÓg.'

Etáin was astounded by this behaviour and she knew that if Eochaidh had seen what had happened he would have had the young man put to death. 'I think you must be mad,' she said, 'coming here, a stranger, and planting a kiss on the lips of the Queen of Ireland. Men have been beheaded for far less. But you are young and I think you are well-intentioned so I'll give you a chance to tell your story. Come away with me before the king arrives.'

And so she took the young man into an ante-room and

there she listened to his story. But it had been many years since Etáin had lived with Midir in Tír na nÓg and though he described to her what it was like and told her stories of their life together she remembered nothing of it. She also found it hard to believe what she heard. How could anyone live for a thousand years?

'I think you must be mixing me up with someone else,' she told him as gently as she could, for she thought that maybe he was a little astray in the head. 'You must go now, before the king arrives. I am married to Eochaidh and I love him. The name Midir means nothing to me.'

But although she enjoyed the party that night, from the moment of meeting Midir a change came over Etáin. Almost every night she began to have strange, unsettling dreams. She dreamt she was in Tír na nÓg and little by little she began to recall what it had been like. Soon her dreams became her reality and she felt like a stranger in Tara. She became restless and unsettled and she hated waking up in the morning and leaving the world of her dreams.

One day Eochaidh was standing on the battlements of his palace when he saw down below a young man with long golden hair wearing a purple cloak and riding a white horse.

The young man got off his horse and knelt before the king. 'I have come to seek your protection,' he said and he rose and saluted the king like a young warrior.

The king made him welcome, as he was obliged to do once his protection had been sought. As they sat together he was struck by the young man's great beauty.

'I have travelled far,' the young man said, 'and I have a longing for a game of chess.'

'I like chess myself,' the king replied, 'but unfortunately the chessboard is in the queen's bedchamber and the queen is still asleep.'

But the young man had his own chessboard, a fine piece of work encrusted with precious stones and he set it up between them and they began to play. Eochaidh won the first game.

'Congratulations,' said the young man. 'Now what do you claim?'

'I'd like you to give me fifty young horses.' Eochaidh said this as a joke and he smiled at the young man, to show him that the High King of Ireland would not take a forfeit from some stranger.

But the young man got to his feet and walked over to the battlements where he stood looking down for a few seconds. 'Your wish is my command,' he said and pointed downwards.

Eochaidh came over and saw down below, grazing in the meadow, a great number of horses, the black sheen of their coats catching the sunlight.

The next game was also won by the king. 'You are an excellent player. What is it you'd like this time?' asked the young man, smiling.

'This time,' said the king, 'I want you to clear that land over there of rushes and rocks and build a causeway over the bog. That way I can help the lives of many of my subjects for that land has always been useless.'

By now Eochaidh knew that he was not dealing with a mortal and he decided that he might as well use the power of the *sidhe* when it was offered to him. So he would make a serious demand that would be of help to the people in his kingdom.

The young man clapped his hands in the air three times and

36

suddenly the land which Eochaidh had pointed out was filled with able-bodied men, hundreds of them, who began to cut the rushes and remove the rocks. Another group of men then started using the rocks to build the causeway. The whole task was completed in two hours. Eochaidh was a little bit afraid for he knew now that this young man, being from the world of the *sídhe*, would have powerful magic which could do anything. When he asked him for a third game the king decided it was better not to refuse. This time it was the young man who won.

'And what do you want? What can I offer you after your generosity to me?' Eochaidh didn't really think that he could offer the young man anything, for though he was High King of Ireland his powers only extended to the mortal world and what could a *sídhe* desire from that?

'There is only one thing I want,' said the young man. 'I want a kiss from Etáin, your wife.'

Eochaidh suddenly felt cold with fear. 'But who are you exactly? How can you ask such a thing?'

'I am Midir the Proud and many years before she became your wife Etáin was mine and we lived together in the Land of the Ever Young.'

Eochaidh was terrified at the prospect of losing Etáin but still he knew that honour bound him to grant the young man his forfeit.

'Come back in a month and you shall have your wish,' he said, playing for time.

The day on which Midir was to return saw the Hill of Tara filled with soldiers from all over Ireland. They guarded the palace in lines ten deep and Eochaidh thought that whatever happened, Midir would not be able to get Etáin through such a cordon. Etáin meanwhile had been waiting for this day and wondering more and more about Midir. Every hour she felt less at home in Tara and was filled with strange longings for another, different life. She had grown listless and sad, with no interest in anything that Tara could offer her.

Suddenly, as it was growing dark and Eochaidh was ordering torches to be lit all around the battlements, Midir appeared from nowhere and stood between the king and queen. He took Etáin in his arms and kissed her, then held her from him. 'At last we are re-united,' he said. 'We can never be parted again.'

With this he tightened his arms around Etáin's waist and together they rose into the air and disappeared.

A howl of anguish went up from the king, and outside the thousands of soldiers standing guard looked up in amazement as two white swans suddenly flew low over their heads, circled the Hill of Tara and disappeared into the cloudy sky. Etáin was finally returning to Tír na nÓg.

THE SONS OF TUAIREANN

❖

The Tuatha Dé Danann could never feel secure in Ireland while they were at the mercy of the Fomorians so King Nuada decided that they would engage in one huge battle and try to defeat their enemy for good. On the morning before the battle, Lugh of the Long Arm was out overseeing the preparations for the fight when he met his father, Cian, heading away from the field of battle.

'Where are you off to, father?' he asked.

'I'm going to round up some old friends of mine,' Cian replied. 'They are all good fighters and brave men. And don't worry—we'll all be back in good time for the battle.'

Cian was nearly as famous a warrior as his son.

The next day Lugh was busy fighting from dawn till dusk and it wasn't until after victory had been secured that he suddenly realized he hadn't seen his father at all since their meeting the previous day. He began to ask around but nobody else had seen him either.

'He must have been killed by our enemies,' one friend suggested.

'Then where is his body?' Lugh asked. 'We Tuatha Dé Danann don't leave our dead lying around on the battlefield—someone would have found my father by now and told me.' He took up his spear. 'Something else is wrong,' he said. 'The last place I saw him was to the north of this spot and I'm going there now to see if I can solve the mystery.'

Taking some of his trusted soldiers with him he set out for the place where he and Cian had met. They walked across the battlefield, which still showed signs of destruction, and on past King Nuada's palace. Suddenly Lugh stopped. 'This is where I said goodbye to my father.' He knelt down and began to examine the spot. 'Yes, I'm sure it was here. And he was heading west, so let us do the same.'

They walked on again, searching the ground for clues and looking around them and calling out.

As they were crossing a rocky field with a wood at the far side and a herd of pigs rooting around, Lugh stopped and held up his hand. 'Be quiet,' he said. 'Listen. I think I heard something.'

As they listened they all heard the same thing—a sort of low moan coming from the middle of the field. They rushed forward and the sound got stronger.

'It's the rocks,' said one of the soldiers in amazement. 'The rocks are talking.'

The terrified soldiers, who feared no living man, now ran back to the edge of the field, leaving Lugh alone.

'Right then,' he said. 'I'm not afraid of a talking rock, so say what you have to say and stop that old moaning.'

'You too will moan when you hear my story.' The voice was coming from the rocks all around, or so it seemed to Lugh. 'Your father, the noble Cian, was crossing this spot when he saw the sons of Tuaireann—Brian, Uar, and Uraca.

40

They were walking towards him with evil in their eyes and seeing that he was outnumbered and remembering the feud between himself and Tuaireann and his family, Cian turned himself into a pig and ran in among that herd that you see still over by the ditch. But Brian, the clever one, identified him and stuck him through with a spear. And your father, not wanting to die in the shape of a pig, turned himself back into a man and those evil brothers took up us stones and they battered him to death and we are stained with his blood for ever more. He lies buried over there under that bit of clay.'

Now, though Lugh was horrified, he was not all that surprised. He knew something must have happened to his father and he knew too of the feud between the sons of Tuaireann and his own clan. It was also well known that Brian was without honour and a vicious coward to boot.

Lugh and his men began to dig around in the clay and soon they came upon a solid mass. Lugh let out a cry of grief as he looked at the bloody, bruised body of his father. There and then he swore vengeance on the sons of Tuaireann.

Some days after this King Nuada was holding a great feast at Tara for all the nobles of the Tuatha Dé Danann and sitting in the feasting hall, eating great gobbets of meat and drinking mead from golden cups, were the three sons of Tuaireann. They were laughing and joking among themselves when in walked Lugh and went straight up to the king's throne.

'What would you do, your majesty, to men who had killed your father?'

'Did someone kill your father, Lugh?' the king asked.

'Yes, and those three men are sitting here now, laughing and jeering about what they have done.'

The king was outraged to hear such a thing and he jumped up and said, 'If it was my father I would find those men and cut off each limb, slowly and painfully, until they died crying out for mercy.'

'I will not do that but I will put a fine on the killers and they will have to pay that fine or die.' Lugh looked round him and his eyes met those of Brian who looked away quickly and buried his head in his golden cup.

There were great murmurings among the nobles with people looking round and many staring straight at the sons of Tuaireann because all knew of the feud between them and Lugh's family.

Brian suddenly jumped to his feet. 'We know what you are thinking, all of you, but I swear to you that our weapons never killed Cian. Nevertheless, just to make you feel better, Lugh, we will pay the fine.'

Lugh smiled. 'Right so. The fine is this. You will bring me three apples, the skin of a pig, a spear, the pup of a hound, seven pigs, a cooking spit, two horses and a chariot, and three shouts on a hill.'

The three brothers looked at one another, smiling in relief.

'Now, do you swear in front of your king that you will pay this fine in full?'

They drew their swords and crossed them and raised them to the king.

'We swear.'

'Then let me tell you this: the apples I want are from the

42

garden in the Eastern Kingdom. They are gold in colour and the size of a baby's head and they are sweeter than honey and their juice can heal all burns.

'The skin of the pig belongs to the King of Greece and it heals all wounds and protects a man from every known sickness in this world.

'The spear belongs to the King of Persia and it is straight and deadly in battle.

'The pigs are those of the King of the Golden Pillar and though they are killed and eaten every night they appear as good and succulent as ever the next day.

'The horses and chariot belong to the King of Sicily and the horses are the fastest in the world and travel on sea and land with equal ease.

'The pup of the hound belongs to the King of Iora and all the beasts of the jungle and the forest fall down in fear before her.

'The cooking spit belongs to the warrior women of the island of Fioncara and any one of them would break your neck with one hand.

'And the shouts must be given on the hill of Miochain where the sons of the king there have taken an oath to kill anyone who shouts on that hill.' As he finished speaking Lugh looked with contempt at the killers of his father. 'Well—there's your fine so off you go and see what you can do.'

Now, though Brian was a nasty piece of work he was also brave and being a son of Tuaireann he had magic powers.

'We can do this,' he said to his brothers. 'Come on, we have no time to lose.'

So, first they set out for the Eastern Kingdom, a peaceful place where visitors were welcome, except for a walled garden in front of the palace that was guarded by young men carrying spears. There were also armed soldiers up on watchtowers around the wall. A big sign said: Keep Out: Private Property by order of the King.

'That's where the apples are, you can be sure,' said Brian and taking out his druid stick he tapped himself and his brothers on the right shoulder and they all turned into hawks that flew up over the wall, plucked a golden apple each with their beaks from the tree in the middle of the orchard and were gone again before the guards even realized what was happening.

'Easy,' said Brian as he dropped his apple in the waiting boat and changed himself and his brothers back into men. 'Now we might as well head for Greece for it's not too far from here.'

'And how will we get the skin of the pig?'

'The Greeks love poetry and poets—we'll go disguised as poets and I'll think of something when we get there.'

They arrived at the court of the Greek king and were allowed in as poets. They had never seen so much gold and glitter—every surface was covered in diamonds and precious stones and inlaid with gold.

'And what brings you young warriors here?' asked the king.

Brian bowed deeply. 'I've written a poem especially for your majesty and I'd like to recite it for you, if I may.'

'Begin,' said the king.

Brian cleared his throat.

> 'In the kingdom of Greece was a king
> Who was ever so fond of his bling

But his pigskin of note
He put in the boat
Of the poets, in exchange for a ring.'

Brian held up a ruby ring and the king of Greece nearly fell off his throne he was laughing so hard.

'You are a cheeky fellow and a hopeless poet but I admire cheek and I'll tell you what I'll do: I won't give you the skin but I'll give you its fill of gold.'

Brian fell to his knees. 'I knew you were a generous and a magnificent king,' he said.

Then the skin was carried out by one servant and a sackful of gold by another four. But before the servants could begin to pour the gold into the skin, Brian had snatched it up and wrapped it round himself.

'Run,' he said to his brothers, and he got out his two swords and began laying into all the warriors around him. In a minute he had killed forty men, including the king. Then, remembering how the king had laughed and admired his cheek, he rubbed the skin across his wound and the king came to life again but was weak still and could only shake his head at the antics of the sons of Tuaireann.

Next they set out for Persia.

'We'll try the poet trick again,' Brian said, 'because it served us well in Greece.'

Arriving in Persia they went straight to King Pisear.

'We are poets of Ireland and would like to recite a poem for your majesty.'

'Whatever,' said Pisear, waving a languid hand, for he was bored with his kingly life. Then he listened to a poem but it made no sense.

45

'What are you talking about? You're just the same as all poets—yacking away and making no sense.'

'It means that I have made you a poem and in return I want your famous spear.'

The king was no longer bored. 'You're dead,' he said, pointing a finger at Brian. But before he could do anything Brian had hurled one of the golden apples. It hit the king on the forehead with such force that it drove his brains out of the back of his skull.

After that it was easy getting the flaming spear and they carried it back to the boat where they stashed it beside the apples and the pigskin.

Now it might be thought that in those ancient days with no emailing or text messages that communications were slow. That was not so, however, and sea birds then carried messages between kingdoms and soon the deeds of the sons of Tuaireann were known everywhere.

So when the King of Sicily heard that they were coming to steal his magic horses and chariot he decided that he would give them up without a fight, which he did, and not one person was killed on the island of Sicily.

The king of Iora was a more headstrong man and he stood his ground to defend the pup but now, between the reputation they had acquired and the apples and the skin of the pig and Pisear's flaming spear, the sons of Tuaireann were invincible and they made short work of Iora and his warriors and carried the beautiful pup back to their boat where she lay down and began to lick Brian's hands.

* * *

Lugh, of course, was well aware of what was going on and how the sons of Tuaireann were becoming heroes throughout the world because of the success of their adventures. He was not happy and he went off to his spell room where he took out his books and made up a powerful spell. Then he went outside and turning east and west and north and south he shook his druid stick in the air and a cast spell on the sons of Tuaireann that would make them forget the rest of the fine and also give them a huge desire to return to their own country.

The sons of Tuaireann fell under the spell and straight away set sail for Ireland, delighted with themselves and the fact that they were bringing the fines back to Lugh. A fair was taking place outside the Royal Palace at Tara and it was here that King Nuada met up with the sons of Tuaireann again.

They showed him the fines.

'You have done well,' said Nuada, 'and we are very proud of you and glad to have you home.'

'But where is Lugh?' Brian asked. 'We want him to have these fines straight away.'

Messengers were sent to find Lugh but when they found him he said that the fines were to be given to the king and that he would show up later.

Now there was great rejoicing at Tara with the news spreading of the return of the sons of Tuaireann and everyone wanting to get a look at the returned heroes. So, the king led the way to a space in front of the palace and the brothers swaggered behind, holding the fines aloft, the little pup, beautiful and quiet as a cat, looking around her with interest.

'What's this then?'

Everyone turned to see who was speaking.

Lugh stood on the ramparts of the palace looking down.

'You've done very well indeed and brought home enough booty to pay any fine'—the sons of Tuaireann looked from one to another, smiling—'but what about the cooking spit? And have you yet given the shouts on the hill of Miochain?'

The brothers stared at Lugh in puzzlement.

'King Nuada here was a witness as were many of the nobles gathered together here today.' He leapt down from the ramparts and stood in front of the three brothers. 'Thanks, lads,' he said, gathering the fines in his arms, 'but I'm afraid you'll have to go back and finish what you started.'

The sons of Tuaireann were in a bad way now. They were tired after all their fighting and travelling and besides, they no longer had the pigskin, the apples, the pup, or the flaming spear to protect them. They went home to Howth to their father but he told them that there was nothing for it but to set out again and bring in the last two fines.

Tired and bad-tempered they set sail for the island of Fioncara. When they drew their boat up on the beach there they found a line of women standing staring at them, their arms folded across their enormous bosoms. One of them came forward and chucked Brian under the chin.

'Well, well,' she said, 'we've heard all about you boys and if we wanted to, any one of us could snap you in half without breaking sweat. However,' she drew a large and dirty finger down Brian's cheeks, 'we sort of like the look of you—don't we, girls?'

There were laughs and giggles and nudges from the

assembled women. 'So we're going to give you the cooking spit—we have plenty more. On one condition.'

'What's that?'

'A kiss from each of you for each of us.'

Afterwards, as the sons of Tuaireann were stowing the cooking spit in the boat, their mouths rubbed red and raw from all that kissing, Uar declared that this had been the hardest fine to win.

'Now we're off to the hill of Miochain and then I'm heading back to Howth and I'm going to sleep for a month. How hard can it be to let out three shouts on top of a hill?'

After two days' sailing they saw the hill, rising up green and steep from the sea. There was no sign of anyone around so they beached their boat and hid it among some trees and decided they would wait until darkness fell before they set out for the hill. They had a bit of a sleep in the trees and later, feeling much better and almost happy now that the end was in sight, they began to creep quietly towards the hill of Miochain.

Slowly, carefully, they threaded their way in the silence and they had reached the foot of the hill when Brian stopped. 'Did you hear anything?'

The others shook their heads.

They started walking again, then stopped as an owl began to hoot.

And from out of the shadows, whooping and screeching, came hundreds of warriors—swords waving, shields shining in the moonlight.

It was a terrible fight and it lasted all night and well into the next morning. But the sons of Tuaireann with their new confidence and their desperation to be finished with all of this, fought as they had never fought before and they laid waste to all around them, beheading men, sticking others through with their spears.

The enemy fell in their hundreds but the sons of Tuaireann did not escape injury and when the battle was over and the warriors were dead or fled, the three brothers lay on the ground, each one with a huge open gash on his chest.

They lay there for several hours as the sun rose in the sky and then began to decline. Finally, Brian pulled himself to his feet. 'Come on, we will give those shouts now,' he said and the three of them hobbled up the hill where they gave the three shouts, their voices weak and quavering.

They rested after that and the next morning they crawled into their boat and let the winds take them home—luckily for them the Atlantic breezes were blowing in the right direction. When they got within sight of Ireland Brian steered the boat around the coast until they came to Howth where some servants of their father's saw them and went running to find him.

He came and looked at his sons, pale-faced, bloody, and near to death.

'Let you go and take this cooking spit to Lugh,' whispered Brian. 'Tell him we've given the shouts but have been badly wounded and ask him for a loan of the skin of the pig. The touch of that skin is the only thing that can save us now.'

So Tuaireann set out to find Lugh and give him the spit and make the request. But Lugh just stared through him, seeing not the man in front of him but the battered, bloody face of his own father.

'The answer is no,' said Lugh. 'Go, Tuaireann, and tell your sons.'

So the sons of Tuaireann died and the feud between the two clans spread throughout the Tuatha Dé Danann and lasted in Ireland for several hundred years, being responsible for much of the bloodshed and death that happened in the centuries to come.

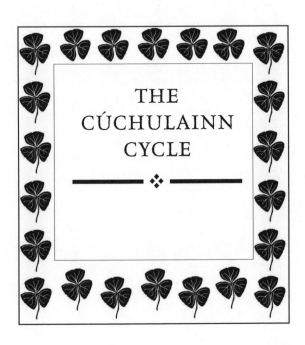

THE CÚCHULAINN CYCLE

HOW CÚCHULAINN GOT HIS NAME

Setanta Mac Sualtam is one of the most famous warriors that Ireland ever produced and he was always extraordinary, even as a small boy. When he was about six years old he went to visit Conchubhar Mac Nessa who was king of Ulster at that time and lived in Emain Machta in a large rath with two hundred young warriors. These young men were famous as athletes throughout Ireland, great hurlers in particular. There were many show-offs among them, fellows who hoped to catch the king's eye.

The morning that Setanta arrived they were idly playing this game on the green in front of the battlements, with one of them trying to drive a ball into a hole while any number—up to ten—defended and tried to prevent the ball going in. The boy watched for a while and then approached a tall blond warrior who seemed to be the leader.

'I'll take the lot of you on,' said Setanta.

The warrior laughed. 'A cub like you. Get out of my sight before I give you a clip round the ears.'

Setanta looked up at him. 'Frightened, are you? I'm not surprised because it's well known that a tow-head is always a coward.'

The warrior was furious and had to be stopped by two of his friends from picking up the boy and shaking him till his teeth rattled.

'Don't you know who he is?' one of the friends asked. 'That's Setanta Mac Sualtam the son of Dechtine, sister of our own king. His uncle loves him dearly so you'd better watch your step.'

But the young warrior didn't care. He had been insulted by a child and he decided to teach him a lesson.

He turned to Setanta with a smile. 'Now then,' he said. 'Let's start with three against one. How does that strike you?'

Setanta just raised an eyebrow and walked slowly onto the white mark in front of the hole from where he was to aim.

Over the next hour the warriors of Ulster found themselves beaten by a child of six and their red faces were due to shame as much as exertion. They started three against one and went up and up and still the boy managed to get his ball into the hole. The warriors ran around him, they jumped up in front of him, and still his aim never failed. One of them even cheated by standing directly in front of the hole but Setanta seemed to be able to curl the ball over his head and find the target.

Conchubhar Mac Nessa had been standing up on the battlements watching all this and now he came down and walked over to Setanta.

'I'm afraid you're too good for them, Setanta,' he said. 'Give the poor lads a break and come with me. I'm off to a great feast that is being prepared for me by Culann. Let's go together. I'd enjoy your company.'

'I'm having too good a time here, uncle,' said Setanta. 'But I'll follow you when I've had more fun.' (The sound that was heard all around Emain Machta then was the sound of the young warriors grinding their teeth.)

'Right you are,' said the king. 'But I'll leave a trail through the forest so that you'll find your way. I don't want you getting lost.'

Conchubhar set out with his royal retinue and after two hours they arrived at the house of Culann.

Culann was the royal smith and that was a very important position because as well as shoeing the horses he made all the weapons for the young warriors who defended the king. He welcomed his master in now, getting his daughters to throw down wild flowers in front of the king as he walked through to the banqueting hall.

There Culann had prepared a great feast. There was venison and wild boar with the tusks still sticking up and huge vats of mead, some cold, some heated to blood heat by a huge iron that Culann had stuck in the vat.

'The hot mead's your only man,' said Conchubhar. 'I've never tasted anything like it before.'

'It's my own invention, your majesty,' said Culann, trying to look modest. 'Here, let me fill you up again.'

By six o'clock the king and most of his retinue were roaring drunk. It was getting dark outside and Culann asked Conchubhar if there were any more visitors coming from Emain Machta that night.

'Divil the one,' said Conchubhar completely forgetting about Setanta. 'What do you want to know for, anyway? Am I not company enough for you?'

'It's not that, your majesty. It's just that I always loose my hound at this time before we go to bed. He is the best guard dog in the whole of Ireland and tonight of all nights I want to make sure that there are no strangers nosing about out there.'

The king waved his consent and with that a huge black dog was brought in on a thick silver chain. When he saw Culann he began to whimper and wag his great tail and when Culann went over to him he began to lick his hands, the tail wagging even faster, causing a mini-storm in the banqueting hall.

'Isn't he a dote?' said Culann with a silly smile on his face. 'I love this dog nearly as much as I love my wife.' (His wife kicked him on the ankle and refilled her goblet with mead.)

'Now, let him out,' Culann said to the servant.

And they all watched as the great hound went lolloping out of the door, opening his huge mouth to show long yellow teeth and howling so loudly that he must surely have been heard down in Kerry.

'I wouldn't like to meet him on a dark night,' said Conchubhar.

'And I'm afraid there wouldn't be much of you left if you did, your majesty,' said Culann. 'He's like a lamb with us here but he's been known to enjoy a couple of strangers as a snack between meals.'

Meanwhile, back in Emain Machta the young warriors had grown tired of being beaten and had all gone home in a sulk, leaving young Setanta alone on the green. Taking up his hurley and ball he set out after Conchubhar, following the trail the king had left behind, the white stones showing up well even in the dark. The woods through which he walked were thick and impenetrable but he had no fear as he skipped along.

He made good time, half walking, half running until he came to the fort of Culann. He slowed down then, crossing the green, throwing up the ball in the air and hitting it with his hurley, catching it and throwing it up again. So absorbed was he in this game that he didn't notice the huge black dog, looking down on him from a ditch, nor notice the redness of its eyes nor the steam coming from its mouth. Its tail was between its legs and its red lips were dripping saliva as it imagined the meal in store.

'Grrrr,' it howled, crouched and then sprang through the air.

But Setanta with lightning-fast reflexes had turned and hurled himself aside. The hound landed on its four giant paws, then turned round too and was facing its dinner once more.

Pawing the ground like a bull, growling deep in its throat, the beast crouched, gathered itself, and sprang through the air again.

But even as it did, Setanta threw up his ball, raised his hurley, and sent the ball spinning through the air right into the open mouth of the hound, with such force that it came out of the back of its skull, scattering skin and brains all over the grass.

The great hound staggered around for a while then, with a long moan, lay down on the ground, dead.

Inside in the fort they had heard the commotion.

Conchubhar, white in the face and suddenly sober, said, 'I swear I will never drink again. Oh, what a terrible thing to have happened.'

Culann's wife looked at him with concern.

'What is it, your majesty? What do you think has happened?'

'It's my sister's boy, little Setanta—he was going to follow me here and I completely forgot about him. Now I fear that he has been devoured out there by your husband's hound.'

At this moment there was a sound at the door—the sound of a hurley knocking against the brass panels.

'Open it,' said Culann.

Two servants did as they were told and there stood Setanta, a hurley in his hand.

'I'm afraid I've lost my ball,' he said.

'*Aii!*' screamed Culann, pointing beyond the boy's head. 'My hound, my pet.' He ran over to where the hound lay dead and began to rub him and pat him. As he saw what was left of his head he turned his gaze back on Sentanta. 'Do you have any idea what you have done?' he asked. 'That dog was my friend. He watched over me and my family, guarded my crops and my cattle, kept us all safe in our beds.' He looked down at Setanta. 'I don't care if you are the king's nephew, I don't care if I lose my job. I want you to go now, Setanta,' he said, 'for you are not welcome here nor will you ever be.'

Suddenly, Setanta didn't seem like a warrior any more but like the small boy he was. 'I am sorry,' he said, running over to Culann and kneeling down in front of him. 'I didn't know he meant so much to you and I feared he might eat me alive. But I give you my word—from this day forth I will act as your guard dog. I will protect your life and the lives of your family; I will watch over your crops and your cattle.'

Cathbad, who was Conchubhar's druid and had come

along with him to the feast, now clapped his hands together. 'Fair's fair,' he said. 'And you've got a good bargain there, Culann. And,' turning to the boy, 'can I suggest a new name for you, seeing what your new duties are going to be?'

'And what name is that?'

'Cuchulainn—the hound of Culann. Hasn't it got a great ring?'

Culann was a fair man and he had to admit that if Setanta hadn't killed the hound, then the hound would have killed him. He also saw that this was no ordinary child and that perhaps he could do everything he promised.

So the child and the smith shook hands, the king forgave Culann the insult to the Royal House, and Setanta became Cuchulainn and was the best protector any man could wish for.

DEIRDRE AND THE SONS
OF UISNEACH

———————— ❖ ————————

Deep in an oak forest in County Meath a little girl
lived with her nurse, Lebhorcham.

The little girl's name was Deirdre and although she
had no other children to play with and never saw another human
being apart from her nurse, she was quite happy.

She befriended the creatures of the forest and had a pet
red squirrel who would jump out of a tree on to her shoulder
when she called him. There were also several generations of a
family of fieldmice who would come and play with her when
she summoned them with a special whistle which she kept for
that purpose.

As she grew older, however, Lebhorcham noticed that her
charge was growing restless; her childish solitary games were
beginning to bore her and increasingly her nurse found her sitting high up in one of the giant oaks trying to see out over the
tops of the trees.

'I wonder what kind of world is out there beyond the
forest?' she began to ask her nurse.

'Never you mind,' Lebhorcham would reply. 'There are

things that you are too young to understand—just take my word for it and be happy here in the forest.'

One day she had not returned home by sundown and Lebhorcham was growing worried, when she walked in the door, her cheeks rosy from the frosty air, her eyes bright with excitement.

'Oh, Lebhorcham,' she said, throwing her arms round her nurse before she could begin to scold her. 'I've had such an exciting time. I followed the blackberry path right to the edge of the wood and I came to a much wider path and there were people passing by, girls of my age and boys and parents with little children. Why do we live here so far from other people? And who are my mother and father that they gave me away to you to mind? Did they die when I was a baby?'

These were the questions that Lebhorcham had been dreading for many years. She looked at her young charge and saw that Deirdre was on the brink of womanhood, a girl of great beauty, graceful and shy as any of the woodland creatures around her. Lebhorcham drew the girl down beside the log fire and began to tell her the strange story of her birth. 'You were born, Deirdre, in the court of Conchubhar Mac Nessa, king of Ulster.'

'A king!' Deirdre drew in her breath in wonder. 'Then am I a princess?'

Lebhorcham shook her head. 'Your father was a man of great talent and learning, a man called Felim, bard to the king.' The old woman poked at the fire, an expression of sadness settling on her face. 'I remember well the night of your birth—in fact I was there at your delivery and it was I who brought the news into the great feasting hall where

Conchubhar and the court were gathered. They were raising a glass to toast your arrival into the world when Cathbad—'

'Who?' Deirdre interrupted.

'Well might you ask, child. Cathbad was a druid and a star-gazer and he had been out in the gardens studying the stars when I came to announce your birth. As I said, Conchubhar was just about to make a toast when Cathbad came flying into the hall, his hair streaming behind him, a wild expression on his face . . . I can see him to this day.' She stopped, her eyes glazing over.

'Go on, go on!'

'"A shooting star fell to earth at the same moment that your wife howled out a final birthpain and gave birth to your first child," he said going up to Felim. "That child is a girl child and she will grow up to be the most beautiful woman in the whole of Ireland. A king will seek to wed her but she will bring great suffering and destruction to the people of Ulster. Many fine young men will die because of her and great sarrow will be brought to this land."

'You can imagine the consternation this caused. Everyone knew what a mighty prophet Cathbad was and how well he read the stars. There were cries of "Kill the girlchild," throughout the feasting hall, "kill her now." Then the king stood up and said that no one would harm a hair on that child's head. "From this moment on," he said, "she is my responsibility. I will hide her away from the eyes of men and I will marry her myself when she becomes a woman."'

Deirdre's face had grown white as she listened to her nurse. 'Oh, what an awful story,' she said. 'Imagine, Lebhorcham, to have it said about you at your birth that you are going to bring sorrow to many people. And to have people shouting that they wanted you killed—and you only a tiny baby.'

Lebhorcham gave the girl a hug. 'There's no need to look so frightened. You've been reared safely in this place and soon I've no doubt the king will come here and soon after that you will be ruling over the court at Emhain Macha. You have a great life in front of you. When Conchubhar marries you, you will be queen of Ulster.'

Deirdre began to smile. 'It might be fun being a queen,' she said.

Knowing who she was and where she came from made Deirdre more content in her forest home. Now she spent the long hours day-dreaming about the time when Conchubhar would come to claim her as his bride and about what her life would be like in Emhain Macha.

'What is it like in the court?' she would ask Lebhorcham.

'Oh, gorgeous, rich and gorgeous. Harpists and musicians play at every meal, wine is drunk from golden goblets and the hangings in front of the great windows are encrusted with sapphires and pearls. In summer there are scented gardens to sit in and in winter whole trees are burned in the huge fireplaces.'

'And Conchubhar? What is he like? Is he handsome?'

But Lebhorcham was less willing to talk about the king, realizing that by now he must be an old man.

One night soon after this there was a heavy fall of snow. Deirdre and Lebhorcham woke up in the morning to a frozen world of great beauty with frost shimmering on the branches of the trees and a white carpet underfoot.

'I'm off to the pond to see if it's frozen hard enough to

skate on,' Deirdre said. Skating was one of the things she loved best about winter.

'Be careful and don't go any further than the pond. You know how near you are to the edge of the forest there and now you know too why you must stay hidden until the king makes you his wife.'

The pond was frozen solid and Deirdre was soon in the middle of it, looping and whirling with grace and speed. She loved skating and was very good at it. But this time she took a turn too near the edge. Her long hair, swinging out behind her, got caught in some brambles, she was pulled backwards and fell down, hitting her head. When she woke out of her faint she found herself cradled in the arms of a young man. She looked at him in fear but then she saw such gentleness and concern in his eyes that she relaxed and listened as he explained to her what had happened.

'My friends and I were out hunting wild boar,' he said. 'We don't usually come this far but the scent was good and it led us here. Then I saw you, lying out there in the middle of the ice and I could see that you must have fallen. I don't think that there are any broken bones but you might catch a chill—I don't know how long you've been lying here. My horse is over there, I'll take you home if you will tell me where you live.'

Suddenly Deirdre remembered what Lebhorcham had said. 'No, I can't let you take me home,' she told the young man. 'I am not supposed even to be seen by strangers. You must go at once now and don't look which path I take.'

'Are you sure you'll be able to manage?' he asked.

'I'm fine.'

Then, as the young man turned to head back out of the forest she called to him. 'What is your name?' she asked.

'I am Naoise,' he replied, 'one of the sons of Uisneach.'

When Deirdre got home she found Lebhorcham in a state of great excitement, standing on a stool cleaning the kitchen window.

'Hurry up,' she said to Deirdre, 'you're really late and there is so much to be done.'

'What's up?'

'The king sent a messenger here to tell us that he is calling to see you tomorrow. Oh, Deirdre—imagine! This time next week I may be helping you to choose a wedding dress.'

That night Lebhorcham washed Deirdre's hair in melted snow water so that it shone with an even deeper sheen. Then she sent her to bed early to be well-rested for the king's visit.

But Deirdre went to sleep with Naoise's name on her lips and that night she dreamt of him. Next morning when she woke up she knew that if she couldn't marry Naoise she would die unwed.

Conchubhar arrived at eleven, making a great deal of noise, sending birds flying through the air in front of him. Other creatures were frightened too by the jingling of his bridle which shone as the diamonds encrusted on it caught the light. He travelled alone for, of course, he wanted no other person to set eyes on Deirdre. The two women watched as he dismounted in the clearing in front of the cottage. Deirdre could see that though he was tall and held himself upright he moved stiffly, like an old man. He shook out the folds of his scarlet cloak and walked up to her. He took her chin in his hand, looked down at her, then stood back.

'You have done your job well, Lebhorcham,' he said. 'Deirdre is more beautiful than any woman I have ever seen. She will make a very fitting wife for Conchubhar Mac Nessa.' He became a bit more human after that and sat down with the two women and drank a goblet of wine and talked gently to Deirdre. 'This day week,' he told her, 'I will return for you and we will go back together to the court at Emain Macha as husband and wife.'

When he had gone Deirdre burst into tears. 'How can I marry him,' she cried, 'he's an old man. Please, Lebhorcham, you must help me to escape.'

Lebhorcham peered around her fearfully as if the king might have been lurking in some dark corner. 'You don't know what you're saying, child. Remember Cathbad's warning and remember that you wouldn't be here today if Conchubhar Mac Nessa hadn't saved you when the men of Ulster wanted you dead. I'll never do anything against the king.'

That night Deirdre lay awake, thinking about her situation. She *was* grateful to the king but she could never marry him. Even if she never saw Naoise again she could not go and live with a man who was old enough to be her grandfather. She didn't sleep at all that night and the next morning she was up and dressed before dawn.

She knew the forest well and had no fear of the creatures that lived there. She let herself out quietly, saluted the barn owl who to-whooed back at her, and went running along the path that led to the pond, crunching the frost under her feet. By the time she got to the pond the sky had grown light and only one or two stars remained.

She looked around her—the place was deserted. She turned away telling herself how silly she had been. 'I'm stupid to think that Naoise would be here—why should I believe such a thing?'

Then, just as she was about to take the path home she heard a horse neighing. 'Come out, whoever you are,' she cried, suddenly frightened, for anyone could be hidden in the trees.

But it was Naoise who came riding out of the forest. His face was red with embarrassment. 'You'll think I'm a fool,' he said. 'I don't even know your name but I could not go home without another glimpse of you. I camped here last night, hoping that you might come back to skate. I wasn't going to show myself—all I wanted was one last look.'

Deirdre and Naoise stood in the middle of the forest, their breath turning smoky in the cold morning air. Deirdre began to talk, telling him about meeting the king for the first time, then shyly admitting that she could never marry as she had fallen in love with—'my rescuer on the ice'.

When Naoise heard Deirdre's story he said, 'I'm filled with joy and with fear. Joy that you feel the same way about me as I do about you, but fear when I think of what Conchubhar Mac Nessa will do when he finds out that he has lost you. Our only hope is to flee together, away from Ulster and from Conchubhar's anger. I'll get my two brothers to come with us, they are single like me and they'll enjoy an adventure, and three of us will be able to protect you better than one. Now, are you sure this is what you want—you may never see Lebhorcham again?'

'Naoise, anywhere you go I will go with you.'

* * *

And so the wandering of Deirdre and the sons of Uisneach began. They travelled first down to Kerry where they thought they might be safe. A mountain chief welcomed them but within a month Conchubhar had discovered where they were and they had to leave. For three more nights they travelled, sleeping by day, wet and cold and hungry, until they came to the kingdom of Ailill, for Ailill had known Naoise as a child and they thought that he might take them in. But their way was barred by ferocious dogs who came barking up to their horses and ran around, teeth bared, until Ailill came out of the palace at Cruachain.

'I'm sorry, Naoise,' he said, 'but I've had enough trouble with Ulster, and Conchubhar Mac Nessa has sent word throughout Ireland that anyone who so much as offers one of you a drink of water will be seen from that moment onwards as his sworn enemy.'

'What will we do now?' Deirdre cried as they rode away. 'What sort of sorrow have I brought to the Sons of Uisneach?'

'Never say that, Deirdre,' Naoise replied. 'As long as you and I are together I am content.'

They decided they would have to leave Ireland and they set off again travelling across the country until they came to a harbour where boats left for Scotland. The next morning they embarked on the journey which took a day and, though Deirdre was sick from the roughness of the sea and cold and tired, her spirits rose when she saw the beauty of the land before her.

'I fought for a chieftain once who has his stronghold ten miles from here. We'll go up there and see if he is willing to let us stay,' Ardan, Naoise's youngest brother, said. He had spent time abroad as a soldier when he had left his father's house.

71

The chieftain made them welcome and even offered them a small house on the edge of a loch. 'My gillie used to live there,' he said. 'But he's dead now and if you care to share the work between you, you can have the house and as many brown trout from the loch as you can eat.'

Deirdre and the Sons of Uisneach felt that at last they could begin to relax. The glen in which they found themselves was well-sheltered and pleasant and the work was easy for three men. Deirdre kept house for the three of them and enjoyed it, remembering all that Lebhorcham had taught her.

But back in Ireland Conchubhar Mac Nessa was growing more and more furious. 'What sort of useless warriors have I got,' he stormed. 'How could you let them escape and where are they now? Ireland is not that big and no one would dare hide them. Find them and don't come back without them.'

Conchubhar wanted to keep his anger on the boil because he was suffering so much from the loss of Deirdre. For years he had looked forward to making her his wife, for years he had dreamt about her beauty. Then he had seen that beauty and just as he was about to make it his own, it had been snatched from him.

As he thought about this he began to feel that he could forgive Deirdre if he could get her back. He could forgive her, but never, not if hell itself froze over, could he forgive the Sons of Uisneach.

Then one morning a young warrior arrived, breathless, with news. 'Your majesty,' he said, 'I've found them. They're living together, the four of them, over in Scotland. And such a life! Everyone over there talks of this happy group who go everywhere together. They swim in the lake now that the weather is improved and play chess at night and Deirdre's laugh rings out and echoes in the mountains all around.'

Conchubhar raised his fists to his forehead and banged it in a fury, causing his crown to fall off. They would all be made to pay for this, they would not get away with it. He began to hatch a plan.

Next day he summoned the bravest of his warriors, a man called Fergus Mac Róich. 'Fergus,' he began, 'I am an old man and I'm feeling older every day. So I've decided that the time has come for me to make it up with the Sons of Uisneach and young Deirdre. I want you to go over to Scotland and tell them that all is forgiven and that I want them to come home—that I've been without them for too long. Can you do that for me?'

Fergus had been Naoise's best friend and that is why Conchubhar had cunningly chosen him. Fergus had missed his friend and was eager now to go and tell him the good news about Conchubhar's generosity, for he believed every word that the king had said to him. 'I always knew you were a good king,' he said, kneeling in front of Conchubhar. 'You are as generous as you are forgiving.'

When he arrived at the loch in Scotland the exiles were delighted to see him for though they were happy in their new life they were often homesick.

'It's lovely to see someone from home,' Deirdre said, offering him a brown trout, crisp from the pan. 'How are things back there?'

'Is Ireland still as beautiful as it always was?' Naoise asked. 'Are the rowan trees in blossom and the apple orchards of Armagh?'

They stayed up late that night, hearing all the news from home. Fergus told Deirdre that Conchubhar had taken Lebhorcham to live in the palace and now she was retired with nothing to do all day but tend the little garden that the king had given her.

'He has a kind heart, after all,' Naoise said.

'He has,' Fergus replied, 'and that is why he sent me over here. He wants you all to come home. He wants to let bygones be bygones. To tell you the truth, I think he's got very old recently.'

'Home,' Naoise sighed. 'It would be great to see Emhain Macha again and all the friends that I left there. What do you think, Deirdre?'

'I think you are crazy to believe such a story. Conchubhar has not forgiven us—this is some sort of plot.' Deirdre knew that the king was too proud to ever forgive them.

But nobody would listen to her and Naoise tried to reassure her, telling her that Conchubhar was kind at heart. 'Anyway, we will be under the protection of Fergus. With Fergus at our side the king will not touch us.'

'And I'll not leave your side, be sure of that,' said Fergus.

When they arrived back in Ireland they were met by a chieftain called Borach whose palace was halfway between Emhain Macha and the coast.

'The king has sent me to welcome you back to Ireland,' said Borach. 'He had hoped to come to my palace to meet you in person and I have prepared a great feast. But now he finds he cannot come. The poor man is getting too old for such journeys. However, he said that Naoise and his brothers and Deirdre are to go straight on to Emhain Macha while I am to entertain you, Fergus. And I'm right glad that someone is going to come to my palace after all the preparations I've made and all the food that has been cooked.'

'It's a trick,' Deirdre said. 'Conchubhar wants to separate us from our protector. Something bad is bound to happen.'

'Look, Deirdre,' Fergus said, 'I'm telling you that you are misjudging the king. He is simply thinking of the great feast Borach has prepared and he is too impatient to see you to allow you to stay here to enjoy it. It's only good manners that I should stay.'

Deirdre still looked doubtful.

'But if you're that worried I'll send my two sons with you to protect you. I can't do better than that now, can I? And stop looking so sad, for heaven's sake. Your face is like a long, wet week.'

Fergus's sons rode on ahead and Deirdre followed in a chariot with the three sons of Uisneach, two of them driving and Naoise by her side.

When they arrived at Emhain Macha all looked peaceful with horses grazing in the great meadow before the palace and little children playing on the lawns. Then Conchubhar came out of the main door and stood on the steps. He raised both arms and called out 'Welcome.' It was a signal he had arranged earlier with his warriors.

Immediately the children playing ran for cover and a great shower of arrows was fired from the narrow windows of the palace. Two found their mark at once and Ardan and Ainnle dropped to the floor of the chariot, dead. For a moment Deirdre thought that Naoise had escaped, then she saw a red stain spreading on his jerkin. She stood up and put her arms around him to support him and as she did another arrow found its mark. This one pierced Naoise's back and reaching right through it pierced Deirdre's breast also, reaching to the middle of her heart. They fell together.

Conchubhar's revenge could not be completed, however, for when he tried to have the arrow drawn out of the two dead bodies so that the lovers could be buried in separate graves, though ten men pulled and pulled and a smithy tried to melt the iron, the arrow could not be budged.

The lovers were buried together and after a while, when Conchubhar was so slumped in depression that he would notice nothing, Lebhorcham planted a little hazel bush on the grave, for the hazel tree was always seen as a symbol of love and loyalty in ancient Ireland.

CONNLA MEETS CÚCHULAINN

———— ❖ ————

When Cúchulainn was a young warrior Conchubhar Mac Nessa sent him to Skye to learn extra skills in war from a woman called Scatha.

She was renowned as a teacher of daring deeds. Although she never left her island and few people had ever met her, her fame had spread throughout the northern lands.

At this time Cúchulainn was already promised in marriage to Emer but while in Skye he fell for the charms of a famous woman warrior called Aoife.

'Aoife,' he said. 'I can't resist you, we must be married.'

So they were and soon Aoife gave birth to a son.

Cúchulainn was delighted. 'We will call the boy Connla,' he said as he took a small gold ring off his little finger and handed it to her. 'When his finger can fit this ring he is old enough to be sent to find me in Ireland. Tell him that when he sets out on his journey he must not step aside for anyone, he must refuse no one in single combat, and he must tell his name to no one. Only when he has been overcome by another warrior is he to declare who he is.'

Exactly seven years after this Conchubhar Mac Nessa and the Ulster warriors were resting on the strand after a morning's hunting when they saw, skimming across the waves, a small boat with a young boy standing up in it. The boy had a sling and from the sling he was firing stones into the air at the birds which flew above him. Each stone brought down a bird and when the bird landed in the boat the boy would revive it and send it up once more into the air. Then he would purse his lips in a whistle and the sound was so powerful and sharp that the bird would fall through the air, stunned, and again end up in the boat. Again it would be revived by the boy who laughed carelessly as he swung his sling over his head.

Conchubhar Mac Nessa had never seen anything like that. 'He's only a child,' he said, 'and look what he can do already. We don't want him landing here in Ulster for I've no doubt that he spells trouble. Which of you will get rid of him?'

Condaire rose, 'I'll have a word with him,' he said. 'He's only a child after all and it will be easy enough to persuade him to be off.'

Condaire stood at the edge of the sea as the little boat was brought towards him on a wave. 'That's far enough, young fellow,' he said. 'This land is ruled by Conchubhar Mac Nessa and he'd like to know who you are and where you come from?'

'Mind your own business,' the boy replied.

'That's a bit cheeky for a child your age.'

'Look,' said the child, 'I don't mean to be rude but I can tell my name to no man. Now, stand aside and let me pass.'

'I'll do no such thing.'

'Are you challenging me? I refuse no challenge but I warn you that if you had the strength of ten thousand warriors you would be defeated by me.'

'Such insults from a cub like you.' Condaire was so disgusted that he turned and walked away.

Up on the beach Conall Cearnach had heard the conversation and being hot tempered and a great warrior he leapt to his feet and went striding down to the boat. 'So, young fella,' he said, 'you think you can insult the warriors of Ulster and get away with it, do you?'

'No problem,' said the child, taking a stone and fixing it in the sling. The stone shot into the air with such a noise that Conall was knocked back onto the sand. And before he could recover, the boy had rolled him over and tied him up with the thongs of his own armour.

Conall was furious as the boy stood over him, laughing. 'Someone do something,' Conall cried. 'How can we be made fun of by this child? It is a disgrace on the honour of the men of Ulster.'

Cúchulainn had felt hot with shame as he watched what the child had done to his friends and companions. Now, with a roar, he ran down and stood towering over the child. 'You've had your fun and games,' he said. 'Now tell me your name and where you come from or I'll kill you dead.'

'As if,' replied the child. 'I've already seen off two of you—why should you be any different?'

'All right,' said Cúchulainn, drawing his sword. 'You've asked for this.'

The boy, in no hurry, also drew his sword. 'If I must,' he said cheekily, then raising his sword he shaved off every blade of Cúchulainn's hair without drawing a drop of blood.

Cúchulainn roared in fury, throwing down his sword. 'Right,' he said, 'we'll wrestle now and see how you do at that.'

'Apart from the fact that I only come up to your knees, I can see no problem.'

With that the boy jumped onto one of two standing stones, made a lasso of his sling, and catching Cúchulainn with it he dragged him in between the standing stones, jumped on top of him and wedged him in there.

Cúchulainn had difficulty freeing himself but as soon as he did the fight was on again. They wrestled into the waves, out into deeper water. Twice the boy held Cúchulainn's head under until he was almost drowning. Then Cúchulainn could take no more. Overcome with fury he grabbed a special magic knife he had and sent it through the waters. It landed on the boy's chest and as it did great barbs opened up and stuck into the boy's flesh so that the water turned red with his blood.

'You've killed me,' cried the boy. 'And that was no ordinary knife.'

'You're right,' said Cúchulainn, 'and I'm sorry. I wouldn't have used it except that I was so maddened by you.' Then he lifted him into his arms and as he did so he suddenly saw his own gold ring on the boy's finger.

'Connla?'

The boy nodded weakly.

Tears streamed from Cúchulainn's eyes, mingling with the seawater. 'I have killed my own son then,' he said.

'It's too late for tears,' said Connla. 'Just point me out the great heroes of Ulster that I have heard so much about that I may say goodbye to them. I had thought that I would join them and become as great a hero as my father but it is too late for that now.'

So Cúchulainn's son bade farewell to the warriors of Ulster and was buried on that strand by them, with the two standing stones knocked into place over the grave. All of Ulster mourned the tragedy but for Cúchulainn it was much worse. For as long as he lived he never really got over what had happened and from that day on he took no delight in fighting or in the feats of a warrior.

HOW THE CATTLE RAID
OF COOLEY BEGAN

❖

Ailill Mac Mata was king of Connacht. He was a strong king, ruling over a wealthy kingdom but most people only thought of him as the husband of Queen Maebh. She was the one whom people spoke about—some in admiration, others in fear. For Maebh was a fierce warrior who let nothing stand between her and her ambition. In fact, she had murdered her own sister to get where she was.

Her husband knew her temper and spent much of his time placating her—telling her how wonderful she was, how strong and beautiful and powerful. He loved her and often wondered how such an extraordinary woman had settled down with him, for though he was a king he was a dull fellow.

This morning, however, he was fed up. Maebh had laughed at him last night in front of all the assembled warriors and had spent the night flirting with other men—something she did to pass the time when she wasn't out fighting. He looked at her asleep, now, so peaceful and beautiful, but he didn't feel his usual rush of gratitude.

I am king of Connacht, I'm a wealthy man, he reminded

himself. Why should I feel humble? Wasn't Maebh the lucky woman the day she captured me? Maebh woke up in a foul humour because she had drunk too much mead the night before. She frowned when she saw Ailill standing over the bed, staring down at her.

'Well—what are you looking at?' she asked rudely, for though she was a queen she had atrocious manners.

'I was just thinking what a lucky woman you were to capture me.'

Maebh leaped out of bed in a fury. 'Why, you skinny-legged, whey-faced creature—I should never have thrown myself away on the likes of you—me, my father's favourite daughter, renowned for my beauty and my fighting prowess throughout the land.'

'Yes, but isn't it great to have such a wealthy husband? Isn't it nice to find yourself surrounded by so much of everything? Your old man isn't exactly a millionaire.'

'What sort of drivel are you talking now? If I'm surrounded by wealth it's my own. Every battle I've fought in I've brought home booty so that now I can guarantee that any earthly goods you possess I can match.'

'Would you like to bet?'

'Call the stewards out and they can start counting. By the end of the week that smile will be on the other side of your face.'

But it took more than a week to count their wealth. First the gold was brought out—his and hers in two different piles. Then the jewels and the weapons and the chariots and the bolts of silk and the wall hangings made from cloth of gold. Then the slave boys and girls, captured in Alban and France.

'How are we doing?' Maebh asked.

'Absolutely equal, your majesty,' a steward replied.

Next they went to the grain stores and after that they began to count the livestock—the horses and cattle and pigs and the herds of deer in the two separate deer parks. The steward came back to Maebh, a look of fear on his face.

'I'm afraid—' he began to stammer and stutter.

'Speak up, you fool. What are you trying to say?'

'King Ailill—'

'What? What about Ailill? Are you trying to tell me that he has something that I haven't got?'

'The bull—the great Finnbheannach.'

Maebh let a roar out of her and threw a spear at the steward, who ducked—you had to have all your wits about you to work in this household.

Then she began to throw goblets and serving dishes on the floor, smashing anything that was breakable, in her fury.

She had forgotten all about Finnbheannach and what made it worse was the fact that he had been her bull originally but had deserted her herd of cattle, preferring to be with Ailill's.

'You—fool,' she said to the steward. 'If you want to keep that head on those shoulders tell me where I can find a bull the equal of Finnbheannach.'

'I don't think—'

'You're not paid to think. Just find it.'

The steward came back the next day. 'There is a bull in Cooley,' he told Maebh. 'A brown bull, as big, as powerful, as noble as Finnbheannach. He's owned by a man called Daire.'

'And you're sure this bull is the equal of Finnbheannach?'

'The only other in the country that is.'

'Then go and tell Daire that Queen Maebh of Connacht

wants that bull. Give him whatever price he's looking for—I don't care how much. I have to have that bull.'

The next morning the steward and a party of warriors set out for Ulster. When they arrived in Cooley the owner of the bull made them welcome and offered them food and accommodation for the night.

'I've a mind to sell that bull,' he said. 'I know he is a noble animal but he has a huge appetite and I can hardly afford to keep him. I'm only an ordinary farmer and maybe the bull would be better off with Queen Maebh's herd.'

But as the night went on and the warriors from Connacht drank more and more mead they became boastful and proud. They looked around them and instead of being thankful to Daire for feeding them and giving them plenty to drink they thought how scrawny his servants looked and how poor his place was.

'Why should our queen pay for his bull?' one of them said loudly, draining his goblet. 'Sure we can take the beast by force if we want to. We could have him back in Connacht in two days.'

The steward told him to shut up but the damage had been done for Daire had overheard their foolish talk. The next morning he summoned the steward. 'Tell your queen that the brown bull stays in Cooley where he belongs. Maebh cannot bribe me with money nor frighten me with the number of her warriors. That bull is mine—now and for always. And tell her further that the men of Ulster wouldn't take kindly to what rightly belongs here going out across the Shannon to the wilds of Connacht.'

That was a bad day for Connacht and a bad day for Ulster. When the steward returned without the bull, Maebh got into one of her furies. Ailill tried to talk sense into her, even offering to share the ownership of Finnbheannach with her.

'Keep your bull,' she said. 'My blood is riz and I'm spoiling for a fight.' (Maebh had never paid much attention to grammar while she was at school.)

So she gathered all her warriors together and set out on a raiding party to capture the bull. 'And I'll call in some favours in the south and the east. That little man won't know what hit him once I get going.'

But before she left she went to visit Fedelm, a seer and prophet that she always consulted before going into battle.

'So, Fedelm—what do you see? My triumphal return with the brown bull?'

Fedelm closed her eyes and threw back her head. When she eventually looked up at Maebh her face had turned a greyish white.

'Well?'

'I see red.'

'What?'

'I see red, only red. Red . . . red . . . '

'Ah, you old fool—I'll have to retire you when I get back.' Maebh shoved her out of the way and was out of the door with a clashing of armour.

But Fedelm was right and the hills and valleys all over Ireland ran red with the blood of Ulstermen and the blood of Connacht men before finally the brown bull was brought west over the Shannon.

Maebh didn't care, she had got her trophy and she slept soundly at night. But many said that it was a high price to pay to satisfy the vanity of a queen.

THE
FIANNA
CYCLE

FIONN AND THE FIANNA

❖

The pipers led in the procession and 'Welcome one and all,' called out the king.

It was the eve of Samhain when the High King, Con of the Hundred Battles, held a great feast in Tara which lasted for six weeks.

Lesser kings and chiefs came from every part of Ireland to drink wine and eat wild boar and roasted wolf, to listen to the music of the harp and to stories told of the olden days, hundreds of years ago, when Conchubhar Mac Nessa ruled and the most famous warrior in Ireland was Cúchulainn.

Con had a band of special warriors called the Fianna. They were brave but quarrelsome and they had a hopeless leader, a man called Goll Mac Morna. Mac Morna inspired no loyalty in his men for all he thought about was feathering his own nest and advancing members of his own family to positions of power.

Sitting at the top table Con said, 'Let the feasting begin and remember that from now until the end of the feast nobody may draw a weapon no matter what quarrels you had last week or last year.'

It was a strange sight in the feasting hall to see so many

fierce warriors sitting there like lambs, many of them with the wounds of past battles not yet healed. There were bloody heads and broken noses and great scars running down cheeks but there was a smile on every face which grew wider as the platters of steaming food were brought in and the mead cup passed round.

Suddenly there was a commotion at the door and a voice said, 'Let me pass.' All heads turned to see a tall young man with white-blond hair stride up the hall and bow low in front of the king.

'Who are you?' asked the king.

The young man drew himself up proudly. 'I am Fionn Mac Cumhaill. My father served you well as head of the Fianna until he was killed at the Battle of Castleknock by Goll Mac Morna.'

Oooh! Breaths were drawn in and heads swivelled in the direction of Mac Morna.

'But,' Fionn continued, 'I come here in peace today and to offer my services to you, Con, and to fight for you in the Fianna like my father before me.' And with that he took off his sword, and kissing the hilt, laid the sword before the king.

When Con spoke there was a tremble in his voice for Cumhaill had been a dear friend of his as well as a brave warrior. 'I remember your father well—he was a good and loyal friend. And I am very glad to welcome you to this feast, Fionn, and to have you in the Fianna. Now,' he beckoned the young man, 'come up here and sit at my table and have a drink of mead for I can tell that you have travelled far.'

The feast of Samhain is always special in Ireland for this is the time when there is passage between the world of the *sidhe* and our world and when the Tuatha Dé Danann come out and mix with mortals. Strange things happen then and sometimes mortal children are stolen by the *sidhe* and fairies left in their place.

In Tara the feasting had just begun. Fionn sat beside Art, the king's son, and everyone in the feasting hall remarked on what a handsome young man he was, and many sitting there had memories of how powerful the Fianna had been under his father. They ate and drank and then sat back, listening to the music of ten harpers.

Then Con stood up to speak and silence fell on the hall. 'You know that tonight at the stroke of midnight the doors between this world and the world of the *sidhe* will be flung open,' he said. 'At that very moment for the last nine years Ailléan of the Flaming Breath has left his rath and come here to Tara and burned my palace to the ground. Nobody can defend it for everyone is lulled to sleep by his fairy music.'

Heads around the feasting hall nodded in agreement and faces grew tense and anxious as they recalled what had happened in previous years.

'Now, I have had enough,' Con said. 'Every year we have to start rebuilding, every year animals are burned alive and last year a little girl, the daughter of one of my servants, lost her life. If any warrior can save Tara from the fiery breath of Ailléan, I will give him any reward he asks for.'

He looked around him but nobody would meet his eyes. The chieftains shuffled their feet and the Fianna looked embarrassed but nobody took up the king's challenge. Then Fionn stood up. 'If I kill Ailléan, can I take up my father's place as head of the Fianna?' he asked.

Con looked towards Mac Morna. 'Well?' he asked him.

But Mac Morna was examining his hands, a sheepish expression on his face.

'Of course you can. For if you slay Ailléan then your rightful place is head of the Fianna.' The king beamed at his new warrior.

Fionn walked out onto the ramparts, closing the doors behind him. It was a bitterly cold night and as he was drawing his cloak around him he heard a whisper from the shadows. He stared but could only make out a black shape.

'Fionn,' said a voice, 'I was a friend of Cumhaill and fought by his side at the Battle of Castleknock. Long have I waited for this day. Here, take this spear, made of silver and embossed with Arab gold. When you hear the music of the *sidhe*, all you have to do is place the blade of this spear to your forehead and you will be able to withstand the magic of the fairy music.'

The shape disappeared back into the darkness so that Fionn could not make out who had been there.

He took the spear and walked to the edge of the ramparts to begin his watch. He did not have long to wait. Two minutes before the clock in the Great Hall struck twelve a mist descended on the countryside in front of the palace. As the clock began to chime, a goblin-like figure rose out of the mist and perched on a stone a few yards from Fionn.

The creature took a silver flute from his pocket and began to play on it. The music was slow, sweet, and melancholy. Listening to it, Fionn found himself beginning to yawn. A weariness began to spread throughout his body and his eyelids grew heavy. All he wanted to do was sleep.

With great difficulty he raised the spear to his forehead and as the cool metal touched his skin he was suddenly alert and full of energy. He watched as the goblin put away the flute and opened his mouth wide. A huge flame came shooting out and began to snake its way towards the wooden doors. But Fionn ripped off his clock, threw it on the flame and stamped it out. Then he turned and made a run at the creature.

The goblin gave a yelp of fear and leapt from the rampart with Fionn after him. He was small and fast and sure-footed but Fionn was fit and had much longer legs. Just as the goblin was about to re-enter his rath, Fionn caught hold of him.

'Now,' he said, 'you've caused enough trouble in Tara. For seven years the king has suffered from your evil deeds but not any more.' And with that he took out his sword and cut off the goblin's head.

Carrying the head aloft he brought it back to Tara where the king and all the warriors were gathered on the ramparts.

'I don't think you'll have any more trouble with Ailléan,' said Fionn as he stuck the head up on the wall for all to see.

'And I don't think I'll have any trouble with my Fianna,' the king replied, 'with you at their head.'

And they all went inside where goblets were raised to toast the new head of the Fianna. Even Goll Mac Morna raised his. 'My reign is over,' he said. 'I'm handing back the leadership of the Fianna to the family of Cumhaill. I know a great warrior when I see one.'

And Fionn took Mac Morna's hand in his. 'Let there be no more quarrels between Con's warriors,' he said. 'Our loyalty is to our king and Ireland and we will pledge ourselves to this cause.'

And Fionn turned out to be the greatest warrior the Fianna ever had.

FIONN FINDS HIS SON

——— ❖ ———

Fionn went out hunting one day on the Hill of Allen near his home. Suddenly his two favourite hounds, Sceolan and Bran, pricked their ears and were off before Fionn could see what they had scented.

When he caught up with them a strange sight met his eyes. On the ground was a beautiful white fawn and the two hounds were licking and nuzzling it.

'Well,' said Fionn, 'aren't you the ferocious hunters!'

The hounds wagged their tails at him and the fawn got to its feet and off the three of them trotted, heading back to the fort, with the dogs on either side, protecting the little fawn.

Fionn took it into the kitchen where he fed it and the two hounds together. Then he left the three of them and went off to bed for he was tired after his day in the open. Sometime during the night he awoke. His room was flooded with moonlight and standing at the foot of his bed he saw a lovely young woman smiling at him timidly.

'This is surely a day of surprises,' Fionn said. 'I can't say I'm not pleased to be visited by such a beautiful creature as you but—how did you get in?'

The young woman began to speak in a soft voice. 'My name is Sadhbh and five years ago a druid of the Tuatha Dé Danann saw me in my father's garden and fell in love with me. When I did not return his love he put a spell on me and turned me into a fawn.

'For five years I have been living in the mountains, fleeing from wolves and hunters. It's cold and lonely up there, as well as dangerous. Then one day I heard that if I could get inside a fort of the Fianna the spell would be lifted and the druid would have no power over me as long as I stayed inside.'

Fionn leapt out of bed and sat the young woman by the fire. 'You poor thing,' he said, 'I've heard how dangerous it is to cross one of the *sidhe* and I'm very glad that Sceolan and Bran found you. Of course you must stay here and I'll do everything I can to make you feel at home.'

Soon they had fallen in love and Fionn asked her to marry him. They were very happy though Sadhbh worried if Fionn was out for long because she never really felt safe without him. So he tried not to go away too much.

But then, one day, he heard that ships from the Northern lands had sailed into Dublin Bay and were getting ready to attack.

'I have to go,' he told Sadhbh. 'It is my job to protect Ireland and the High King. You'll be fine so long as you stay inside the fort.' And he kissed her and was gone.

The Fianna were away for two weeks, for the Norsemen put up a good fight. When they returned Fionn ran into the fort calling out Sadhbh's name.

A servant came out, her face pale. 'She's gone,' she said.

'What do you mean—gone?'

'Last Sunday she was standing looking out for your return as she did every day since you left. Suddenly she saw a man in your shape with two hounds running around him, exactly the same as Sceolan and Bran. She ran out before I could stop her for I feared some trickery. When she got to the man he struck her with a hazel wand and she disappeared. The next thing I knew a lovely white fawn came running towards me, trying to get back into the fort but the two hounds, yelping and howling, chased her away and off into the hills.'

'So that's it,' said Fionn sadly. 'The wretched druid has tricked her again. I should never have left her alone for so long.'

For the next seven years, Fionn went searching throughout Ireland for Sadhbh. He searched every mountain and valley and he took Sceolan and Bran with him for he knew that they would protect the fawn until it could be brought back safely to the fort. Finally he admitted to himself that he would probably never see Sadhbh again and with a heavy heart he decided to give up searching.

To try and forget her he threw himself into his old pursuits, especially hunting which he had loved so much. One day up high in Ben Bulben, the hounds had gone on ahead into a deep thicket when they suddenly set up a fierce racket, barking and snarling.

'Let's see what they've found,' Fionn said, getting off his horse and beating his way through the thorny growth with his sword. He came out into an opening to find the hounds circling round a young boy who stood naked and with hair down to his waist. Though the hounds were baying and salivating with bare teeth, the boy seemed unafraid. And then Fionn's heart leapt in his chest as he noticed that Sceolan and Bran were standing guard on the boy, keeping the other hounds back. He was reminded of that other time when they had protected the white fawn. 'Can it be?' he wondered, joy flooding into his heart. 'Could it possibly be . . . ?'

Fionn put the boy up on his horse and they rode back to the fort together. When he got him home he gave him a bath and put him to bed and when he was comfortably settled he took him a bowl of porridge and cream.

'Now, can you tell me something about yourself?' Fionn asked.

It was then that he discovered that the boy could not speak.

Fionn kept the boy beside him and was very gentle and undemanding. Soon he was making human sounds and little by little he began to speak. Then one day he was able to tell his story.

'My home was a cave high up in a mountain overlooking the sea,' he said. 'It was a very wild place and nobody ever came there.'

'Your parents?' asked Fionn.

'I didn't have any. I was reared by a white hind who showed me where to find berries and nuts and where to find spring water. She kept me from danger and I had many friends among the wild creatures of the mountain—goats and eagles and a wild cat that used to let me play with her kittens. It was a happy life except when we were visited by this dark man. The hind was afraid of him and would run into the cave and hide me away when he came.'

Fionn shook his head. 'I can make a pretty good guess who that was.'

'One day,' the boy continued, 'he arrived when we were sitting resting in the sun. Before the hind could do anything he had struck her with a hazel rod and chased her down the side of the mountain. I tried to follow but he kept me back. It was when I was looking for her that your hounds found me.' The young boy stopped talking and looked up at Fionn.

There were tears in Fionn's eyes as he put an arm around the boy. 'Why didn't I see it before?' he asked. 'When I look into your face I see Sadhbh's beautiful features. You are my son. Welcome home, little fawn. Welcome home, Oisín.'

And that is how Fionn found his son and how Oisín got his name—Oisín, little fawn.

OISÍN IN TÍR NA NÓG

— ❖ —

O f all the young men in the Fianna, Oisín was the most famous, not only because his father was Fionn Mac Cumhaill but because he was such a brave warrior and such a talented poet.

Any time he had a few minutes free he would start to think about a poem he could write.

Soon his fame had spread throughout Ireland and women who were quarrelling with their husbands would say, 'If only you were more like Oisín, brave as a lion and still soft and tender enough to sit down and write a poem.'

One day after a morning's hunting Fionn and Oisín and the rest of the Fianna were lolling on a bank, resting their horses and letting them drink from a fast-moving stream that came gushing down the side of a mountain. The sun was shining on the water and as Oisín looked, a rainbow appeared and from out of the rainbow a horse and rider began to materialize.

He blinked, wondering if he was imagining things, but the horse continued to prance forward.

As they came closer Oisín saw that it was a very fine animal, snow white but with a most unusual red mane. He moved his gaze upwards and then he forgot about the horse as his eyes were dazzled by the rider. A beautiful young woman sat straight as a hazel rod in the saddle. Her hair was the colour of the gold coins in his purse and it reached down to her waist. The horse didn't seem to gallop so much as float down towards them. Fionn stood up.

'You're a stranger in these parts,' he said. 'Indeed few people, particularly young women, come to such a lonely place. Are you lost?'

The young woman shook back her hair. 'Indeed I'm not, Fionn Mac Cumhaill—Ah yes, I can see that you are startled that I know your name.'

'I certainly am,' replied Fionn, 'when I don't know yours.'

'My name is Niamh of the Golden Hair and I am the daughter of the king of the Tuatha Dé Danann.'

The brave warriors of the Fianna drew back in fear for everyone knew of the magic powers of the Tuatha Dé Danann.

Fionn however, did not flinch. He bowed respectfully to her—after all she was a princess—and said, 'Well, Niamh, you are most welcome to Ireland. Did you come for any particular reason?'

'I came because I had heard about your son Oisín. For many years now my father has tried to find me a husband from among my own people but I didn't fancy any one of the men that he produced for me. I began to think that I'd never get married and then I heard about Oisín, how he was such a great warrior and such a talented poet. I suppose you never realized that your son's fame had spread as far as Tír na nÓg?'

'I certainly did not,' Fionn replied, not knowing whether to be pleased or not.

'I liked what I heard about him and so I came looking for him. And now that I've found him I realize that as well as his other qualities, he's very good-looking.' She turned in the saddle and looked down at Oisín, offering him a most dazzling smile. Oisín blushed. What with that smile and the compliments she had paid him, he knew that he could not withstand the charms of this young woman. He looked up at her and felt himself bewitched.

'I want you to come back to Tír na nÓg with me,' Niamh said. 'When we get there we will be married and you cannot imagine the fantastic life we'll have. My father will give you lands and castles to rule over and I will love you like you've never been loved before.'

Oisín began to move towards her but Fionn put out a hand to stop him. 'Please, son,' he said, 'think again. I've never heard of any mortal returning from Tír na nÓg and I am an old man now. I lost your mother, I don't want to lose you too.'

But Oisín was deaf to such pleas. Taking Niamh's outstretched hand he jumped up behind her. 'Don't worry,' he said to his father, 'I'll be back. But I cannot deny the call of true love.'

He put his arms round Niamh's waist, the white horse kicked up his heels, and off the three of them went, back behind the rainbow.

Niamh's was a magic horse that travelled with equal ease over land and sea. Soon they arrived at a high wall of banked cloud and when the horse neighed the cloud parted and Oisin saw before him a land of vivid colours where the grass seemed greener, the sky bluer, and the corn in the fields more golden than in Ireland.

'Welcome to Tír na nÓg,' said Niamh. 'I can promise you that you will never regret your decision to come with me.'

She took Oisín to meet her father the king and to introduce him to all the nobles and the servants who lived in the palace. The first thing Oisín noticed was that nobody was old and nobody was cross. Everybody seemed in such good form as they rushed around full of energy. 'Everyone seems so happy,' he said.

'Why wouldn't they be,' replied the king. 'Nobody has any worries in Tír na nÓg.'

Niamh and Oisín were married and Oisín settled down quickly to his new life. He loved to be out in the open in this beautiful country where the sun always shone but never too fiercely, where a gentle breeze blew in the afternoons. When it blew from the west it smelled of the sea, then when it changed direction and blew from the east it brought with it the perfume of wild herbs.

Wild flowers grew in abundance everywhere and the ditches were full of strawberries, big as plums, the hedgerows full of hazel nuts. If you felt like salmon for your dinner all you had to do was stand at the mouth of a river, voice your desire, and the fish would leap out at your feet.

At first Oisín was deliriously happy. Niamh was as good as her word and she made a great wife, ordering the servants to bring him breakfast in bed and always ready to laugh at his jokes and listen to his stories about life in the Fianna.

But after a while Oisín began to worry about his father and as he talked about the Fianna he remembered what a close band of warriors they had all been. He began thinking that maybe it had been selfish of him to go off like that and leave them, particularly as his father was not a young man. He didn't want to return to Ireland too late and find that Fionn had died.

'I must have been here about three years now,' he said to Niamh one day. 'I think I'll go back to Ireland—just for a visit mind—and see how everyone is getting along.'

Niamh's heart was gripped with fear for by now she really loved Oisín. 'If you go, you'll never come back—I know. Stay here with me, Oísin, this is your home now.'

But Oisín grew sad and Niamh could see that there was no point in making him stay against his will. Though she feared what might happen she felt she had to let him go back to Ireland for a visit, otherwise he would just grow more depressed.

'All right,' she said. 'I'll help you. You can have my magic horse—that way you won't get lost between one world and the next, for that horse knows the way to the world of mortals like he knows his own paddock.'

Oisín gave her a smacking kiss on the mouth. 'Oh thank you, Niamh. You are the best wife a man could have and I'll be back to you before you even notice I'm gone.'

'Only remember—don't get off the horse. If you get off the horse you can never return to Tír na nÓg. If so much as one of your toes touches the soil of Ireland you will never see me again.'

Oisín set off in high spirits. The little horse seemed to travel even more quickly than on the first journey. When he got to the bank of cloud, he neighed, the cloud opened and they floated over the sea and soon they arrived in Ireland.

The little horse set out along a stony road with farmland on either side. 'What!' Oisín said in disgust, looking round him. 'What has happened to this country? Where are the fine forests we used to hunt through? And what are those funny little hovels—do people actually live in them? I don't like the look of this one bit.'

He decided that things might look better nearer home and he ordered the horse to head straight for the Hill of Allen and Fionn's fort. Soon he began to recognize the outline of the hill and he urged the horse on faster. 'We're home,' he said. 'The fort is up—' He broke off and looked up in amazement. The hill was in front of him but there was no sign of a fort. He urged the horse upwards and slowly began a search, thinking that he had forgotten the position of the Fianna's stronghold. Nothing was to be found however, not even a ruined building. The whole hill was covered in coarse bracken that caused Oisín to sneeze.

'I'm totally flummoxed,' he said to himself. 'Even if Fionn and the Fianna decided to move on somewhere else, surely there would be some trace of their strongly-built fort? This makes no sense at all.'

He turned the horse and began to make his way back down. When they were nearly at the bottom of the hill he saw a shepherd with a flock of scrawny sheep. For a moment Oisín was surprised by the man's appearance—he had forgotten what old people looked like.

'Excuse me,' he said, 'I'm looking for Fionn Mac Cumhaill. His fort used to be up there on the Hill of Allen. I can't understand that there is no trace of it. Have I come to the wrong place?'

The shepherd stood up and shook his crook at him. 'Be off, young fella,' he said, 'and stop trying to make a fool of your elders. Have you come here to mock me? You know as well as

I do that Fionn and the Fianna have been dead this three hundred years. Are you trying to pretend that I am three hundred years old? Just because you're a fine young fellow doesn't mean that you won't grow old one day and lose your teeth like me. Now, get out of my sight and stop annoying me.'

The fellow was doting, Oisín decided, urging on his horse. They trotted on until they rounded a bend on the track they were following. Some men came into sight. They were gathered together in a bunch as they tried to heave a boulder into a field. They pushed it and pulled it but they couldn't budge it.

Oisín looked at them—scrawny creatures! He looked at the boulder—he would have no trouble moving that on his own.

He rode up to them. 'Afternoon, men.'

They nodded civilly enough.

'Here,' said Oisín, 'let me give you a hand.'

He leaned over, stretching down to try and reach the boulder. As he did, however, the horse's girth broke and Oisín found himself sliding towards the ground. Remembering Niamh's warning he tried to stop himself but he couldn't regain his balance.

As soon as his foot touched the earth, the horse reared up and shook him off completely. Then it seemed to rise in the air and disappear skywards. The workmen, amazed by the disappearing horse, turned back to look at its rider. A shudder of fear ran through them as they saw huddled at their feet a wizened, wrinkled, bald-headed old man instead of the handsome young stranger who had stopped to help.

'Don't go near him,' somebody said. 'Send for the holy man. He's not afraid of magic.'

'Send for the holy man,' the cry went up. 'Send for Patrick. Patrick will know what to do.'

When Patrick came he picked Oisín up tenderly and took him back to the simple cell he was living in. There he looked after him until he died a week later, the oldest man who had ever lived.

He was over three hundred years old—the last brave warrior of the Fianna.

A QUARREL AMONG THE FIANNA

❖

You could say that the Fianna fought hard and played hard and when they weren't out hunting or fighting they liked nothing better than a good party.

Fionn Mac Cumhaill thought it was time to do some entertaining so he sent out an invitation to all the Fianna and their friends and relations inviting them to a great feast to be held in Allen.

Everyone was invited and everyone came—Fionn's son Oisín and his son Oscar, Goll Mac Morna and all the clan, Caoilte MacRonan, Diarmuid—everyone.

Fionn sat at the head of the table and gave the place of honour opposite him to his old friend Goll Mac Morna. They had been comrades in arms for many years, with Goll always watching out for his leader. They were fond of one another, though, being warriors, they never showed it.

The Hill of Allen looked splendid under a new moon. Whole animals were roasted in pits outside and cut up and brought into the banqueting hall on great wooden platters. Whole apple trees had been stripped to provide fruit for the pies and fifty cows milked for the cream. In front of every guest was a golden goblet which busy servants kept filled to the brim with mead.

111

After they had eaten and drunk and talked and laughed, Fionn put up a hand. 'I hope everyone is enjoying himself,' he said, 'and has had his fill of food and drink?'

There were cries of assent and the clinking of goblets.

'You have surpassed yourself tonight, Fionn,' said Goll Mac Morna. 'This is the best feast I have ever been at.'

Fionn looked at him affectionately. 'Thanks for that,' he said. 'But now I want you all to sit back and I'll ask Fergus to recite a poem to entertain us.' It was the custom in noble Irish households and had been for many years for the resident bard or *file* to recite a poem or two at a feast, usually in honour of his master.

Fergus was the bard of the Fianna and he stood up now and began to sing of the great deeds of Fionn and his ancestors, of their bravery in battle, their integrity and generosity. When he had finished, Fionn stood to thank him, and then he and his sons began giving him the most amazing and costly presents— the other guests gasped at the wealth they saw heaped up in front of the *file* and even Fergus himself was astonished.

'You are too generous to me,' he said. 'Here, let me give you another poem.' This time he began to sing about the Mac Morna clan and their deeds in battle and their valour.

Goll Mac Morna, who could never really hold his drink, started to preen himself and look proud and as soon as the *file* sat down he leapt to his feet and said, 'You're in luck, Fergus, for I've just collected my tribute from Norway so I'm flush and I'm feeling generous.'

He clapped his hands and his body servants standing beside his chair ran out and came back with several sackfuls of precious stones and gold and silver ornaments and coins.

These Goll now began to shower on to Fergus's lap, making what had seemed like Fionn's munificence now appear as just a few baubles. And not content with that, when he was finished dishing out the goodies to Fergus, Goll went swaggering around the banqueting hall giving gifts to everyone he met— musicians, jugglers, servants, doling them out like marbles.

'Here, have another armlet,' he said to a magician. 'Plenty more where that came from'

A disapproving silence fell on the room and at the top of the table Fionn's face was pale and frowning. Everyone was embarrassed by Goll's behaviour, trying, or so it seemed, to outdo his host and trying to impress everyone with his wealth. The whole display was over-the-top, even vulgar.

Fionn's voice was full of anger when he spoke. 'Remember your place, Goll,' he said. 'You are here as my guest, so please sit down.'

But Goll had been drinking all evening and didn't notice the edge to his old friend's voice. 'Relax, will you?' he said, smiling and lifting his goblet in a mock salute. 'Can't a fellow be generous if he's in the mood?' He poked a finger at Fionn. 'It wouldn't be that you're jealous, would it now, Fionn?'

Fionn face turned from white to red. 'I would not let you get away with such a comment,' he said, 'but I have with me a hundred men for every one you have and I would never take advantage even of a Mac Morna.'

Goll laughed and emptied his goblet, holding it out for a refill. 'Maybe we could add cowardice to jealousy—what do you say to that?'

Before Fionn could reply, his brother Cearabhaill, letting out a great war-cry, had leaped to his feet and thrusting his face centimetres from Goll's, said, 'You dare to say such a thing to the great Mac Cumhaill—you, one of the mongrel breed of Mac Morna who are well known for hiding behind the skirts of your women folk when you hear the rattle of a shield.'

This was such an outrageous lie that Goll just started laughing but his brother Conan, more impetuous (and a good bit dimmer), felt the insult to his whole family and jumped in front of Goll, raising his fists and squaring up to Cearabhaill. 'You half-witted creature, if you weren't such a fool I'd take my sword to you for such talk,' he said.

'You bald-headed weasel, we'll soon see who's the fool,' Cearabhaill said and landed a blow on Conan, just under the chin.

Conan hit him back, his huge fist bashing into his nose, and as the blood began to trickle fighting started to break out all over the room. Two of Oscar's sons rushed to defend their uncle and two of Conan's sons joined in on the other side. Furniture was overturned, crockery was broken, and blood began to flow from wounds, some serious, some slight.

The only two people left sitting in the hall were Fionn and Goll. They looked on at the melee in front of them but neither spoke and their two faces were completely without expression.

Just then another of Fionn's sons came storming into the hall followed by a hundred Fianna warriors and these soon forced all the Mac Morna clan outside where the fighting continued.

As soon as this happened, Fionn looked at Goll and Goll looked at Fionn and in silent agreement both men reached for their body armour. One after the other they strode out to join in the fighting.

They say that a fight among friends is far worse than one between enemies and that was so now. Used to fighting together the Fianna warriors now turned their weapons and their anger on each other with a ferocity that soon left bodies strewn around on the grass. Swords and spears were cutting into flesh and groans and cries were sounding from all around. The grass, green a few minutes ago, was now a brownish red.

Fergus, looking on in horror, knew that he had to do something. He summoned all the *fili* and bards of the Fianna and they formed a chain around the fighters and began to chant and sing, clapping their hands and stamping their feet, the rhythm insistent and dominant. As their voices rose they drowned out even the noise of battle and the warriors, gradually becoming aware of the sounds coming from the *fili*, began to turn from the fight, dropping their weapons on the ground. It was as if the chanting and stamping was having a tranquillizing effect on them.

'Enough, then,' said Fergus. 'Let you stop this fight between old friends. Stop it now before the entire Fianna is wiped out.'

'Agreed,' said Goll, fingering his black eye. 'Bygones be bygones, Fionn?'

'Not so fast, Goll,' said Fionn. 'I want this matter adjudicated by the High King, for a lot of blood was spilt today. Let him decide the rights and wrongs of it and I'll abide by what he says.'

The whole of the Fianna set out for Tara and the court of Cormac Mac Art. The king was used to adjudicating in all sorts of disputes and now he called together seven wise people, including his daughter, Ailbhe, and asked them to sit in judgement and listen to the evidence with him. Before the proceedings could begin, however, Goll stepped forward and bowing low said, 'I object to Fionn giving evidence to your majesty.'

'And why is that?' asked Cormac.

'Because he is prejudiced against me and will not speak fairly.'

'Then who do you want to speak?'

'Fergus. He will be fair to both of us for he is a *file* and beyond reproach in even-handedness.'

So Fergus was asked to step forward and he gave his evidence truthfully, describing what had happened: that Fionn's brother had struck Conan Mac Morna, that Conan's son had gone to the assistance of Conan and Oscar's sons to the assistance of their uncle and then that the clan Mac Morna and the clan Mac Cumhaill had joined in on either side and after that everyone else joined in too.

It had been a bad business, Fergus said, with what started out as a minor brawl ending in a battle in which eleven hundred of Fionn's people and sixty-one of Goll's had been killed.

'I find it very surprising that considering the number on Fionn's side, so few Mac Mornas were killed,' said the king.

Fionn blushed in shame. 'I was pressed in myself,' he said. 'There was such a weight of warriors that I couldn't get out or—'

'Or?' Goll questioned tauntingly.

'Lads, lads,' Fergus intervened. 'Hasn't enough damage been done?'

The king sat down on his throne and the other judges gathered around him. He turned to the first judge. 'What's your judgement?' he asked.

'I find for the Mac Mornas,' was the answer.

'Why?' asked the king.

'Because they were attacked first.'

The king shook his head. 'Fionn is the head of the Fianna and every single man owed him allegiance above and beyond loyalty to the clan—you've forgotten that.' He then asked the second judge for his opinion.

'I too find for the clan Mac Morna but as to damages, I think that with so many of his warriors killed, Fionn has already paid the price. There should be no more to pay, no fines of any kind and that is my judgement.'

'And I agree with you,' said Cormac.

Fionn and Goll accepted the judgement of the court and they touched foreheads, which was the way the Fianna showed friendship and forgiveness. They walked back to Allen together, arm-in-arm, and though Fionn was still annoyed at Goll's behaviour and especially at losing so many of his men, he remembered what a good comrade Goll had been to him down the years, how he was always there, at his elbow when he needed help.

'Bygones,' he said, slapping Goll on the back.

'Bygones,' echoed Goll and the two warriors linked arms once more, each one silently swearing that never again would he be responsible for the spilling of Fianna blood.

THE STORY OF DIARMUID AND GRAINNE

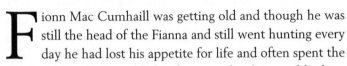

F ionn Mac Cumhaill was getting old and though he was
still the head of the Fianna and still went hunting every
day he had lost his appetite for life and often spent the
evenings chewing on a blade of grass and sighing and looking
into the distance.

'I know what you need, father,' Oisín said to him one day.
'You need a new wife, for you have not been the same since
the death of Maighneis.'

'I'm an old man,' said Fionn, running a hand across his
thin, white hair.

'But still a very handsome one,' replied Oisín.

'You're right there,' said Fionn, perking up. 'I've held on to my
fine figure and my looks. Maybe a new wife is just what I need.'

'And I have just the girl for you.'

'You have?'

'Grainne, the daughter of the High King. Not only is she
beautiful but she's said to be intelligent too and very high
spirited. Now—will you come with me to Tara and we can
sound out the High King?'

Suddenly, Fionn looked shy—you could almost see a blush rising in his withered cheeks. 'Would you go by yourself?' he asked Oisín. 'Would you go and put my case to Cormac? I'll wait here and hope for the best.'

So Oisín and a group of the Fianna set out for Tara where they were made very welcome by Cormac, the High King.

'So, lads, what brought you to these parts?' the king asked after their hands had been washed in rosewater and their thirst quenched with goblets of mead.

As Oisín began to explain their quest, a gleam came into Cormac's eye. Fionn Mac Cumhaill was no longer a young man, it was true, but he was still the bravest and the best warrior in the whole of Ireland. Besides, Grainne was a bit of a handful—headstrong and determined always to have her own way. She had already turned down seven men who had come seeking her hand in marriage, on each occasion demanding a new cloak from her father to make up for her disappointment.

Cormac looked at Oisín. 'Let you go over to the women's house now and tell Grainne what you've come about. If I make an appearance she'll just see it as me interfering in her life and she won't have that.'

To everyone's surprise, Grainne agreed to marry Fionn and set out to meet him the next morning with a retinue of her maidens. 'You stay here, father,' she commanded the High King. 'I'm only going to seal the bargain but I'll be back within twenty-four hours when I'll be looking for gold from you—as you well know I haven't a stitch to wear.'

So they set out for Kildare and reached the Hill of Allen before nightfall. Fionn was seated at a fire, with the light from it shining on his wrinkles so that he seemed even older than usual. Around him were dozens of the Fianna, resting now after their day's hunting, handsome young men who looked Grainne up and down as she passed by them. She, however, had made up her mind to marry Fionn and, paying no heed to any of them she swept across to Fionn and extended her hand to him, which he kissed gallantly (for he had had plenty of practice).

That night a great betrothal feast was held in Allen. Grainne, as the daughter of the High King, had brought casks of her own mead, made from the honey bees that were confined to the Hill of Tara. She herself began pouring it, walking around among the Fianna, smiling graciously and offering a word here and there.

When she came to Diarmuid Mac Dhuibne—Fionn's favourite young warrior—she did notice how handsome he was with his dark curls and flashing white teeth. But she was now engaged to Fionn and she would have passed Diarmuid by except that as she was filling his goblet she tripped and in steadying herself she accidentally knocked off the cap that he was wearing.

'Sorry,' she said, bending to retrieve it. 'Let me—' She stopped and stared and then began to feel a strange wobbly feeling in her tummy. 'Oh Lord,' she said, swallowing hard. And, 'Oh Lord,' again. Her eyes were fixed on Diarmuid's face and the smile spreading on her lips could only be described as soppy.

Diarmuid snatched the cap from her hands and pulled it well down on his forehead. But the damage had already been done for Grainne had seen the lovespot (a small dark mark like a large freckle, just above his left eyebrow) and like every woman who gazed on it she had fallen madly in love with

Diarmuid. This was why he kept the cap on at all times and he thought what bad luck was his that it should have been knocked off in such a fashion by the future wife of his leader.

'Be off with you,' he whispered angrily, not wanting Fionn to hear but desperate to be rid of Grainne. 'You leave me be for I want to have nothing to do with you.' He walked away from her but she just smiled lovingly at his back and sighed in a lovesick manner.

Later that night after they had all eaten and drunk their fill, Grainne stood up at the table and ordered one of her maidens to bring out a new cask of mead. 'This is very special wine, dear Fionn, and I want you and all your warriors to drink a special toast—to the happiness of all women.'

Again she went round pouring out the mead, though when she approached Diarmuid he turned his back on her, which was what she wanted.

Then the Fianna, apart from Diarmuid who was now skulking behind a tree, raised their goblets, drank the toast, and fell down where they stood in a deep sleep.

Immediately Grainne ran over to Diarmuid. 'Now, I've spiked their mead and they'll all sleep for hours, which will give us the chance to get right away.'

'Are you mad?' Diarmuid asked. 'I'm going nowhere with you.'

'But I love you madly.'

'That makes no matter. You are promised to Fionn and Fionn is my leader and a man that I respect and love above all others.'

'Poppycock,' said Grainne, coming out in her true colours. 'I'm in love with you and you should count yourself lucky.

Remember that I'm the daughter of the High King and I am doing you a great honour but—' the silly smile was on her lips again, 'you are very handsome. Come on now, hurry up, and let's make our getaway while that lot is snoring there.'

'I said—I'm going nowhere with you.'

'You will because I now put you *faoi geasa*.'

To be put *faoi geasa* meant that Diarmuid was obliged to do as Grainne asked and so, reluctantly, he followed her and her maidens, leaving Allen and the Fianna behind, feeling full of shame and sorrow.

And that's how the wanderings of Diarmuid and Grainne began for from that day they became hunted creatures.

When Fionn woke up and discovered what had happened he was filled with fury and vowed that he would not stop till he had tracked down the lovers and killed either one or both of them, depending on the mood he was in. He and the Fianna followed them up and down the length and breadth of Ireland, sometimes missing them by a day, sometimes only by minutes. He had spies throughout the country on the lookout for them and they could never sleep in one place for more than one night nor eat a meal in the same spot twice.

He went to a druid to ask him to put a spell on Diarmuid that he might lose all his strength and die of a lingering sickness but the spell didn't take and Fionn heard that Diarmuid was stronger than ever, out hunting every day, providing food for himself and Grainne.

Then, after several years, Fionn seemed to lose heart and he said that he would hunt the lovers no more and agreed that they might settle down somewhere so long as it was far away from him and far too from Tara.

So Diarmuid and Grainne at last found a home in Rath Grainne in County Sligo where they lived for sixteen years and had four sons and one daughter. They were very happy but Grainne sometimes thought about the old days and one morning she said to Diarmuid, 'Now that Fionn has forgiven us I would like to invite him here to this place and my father too for they are both old men and I would like to see them before they die. Why don't we make a great feast and invite them both?'

Diarmuid, knowing Fionn's character, was reluctant to agree but he did in the end because he could deny Grainne nothing.

So a party from Tara and many warriors from Allen with Fionn at the head set out for Sligo where they were entertained with feasting and drinking and juggling and spell making. The feast lasted for a day and a month and everyone said that its like had never before been seen in Ireland.

On the last night Diarmuid and Grainne went to bed exhausted and glad that the guests would be leaving tomorrow. But they had only been asleep for a few hours when they were woken up by the sound of a hound, its baying coming loud and lonesome in the middle of the night.

'I have to go and find that hound,' said Diarmuid. 'It's driving me crazy and I'll have to go and shut it up because otherwise I know I won't go to sleep tonight.'

But Grainne persuaded him to stay where he was because she thought it was the Tuatha Dé Danann out making mischief on Ben Bulben.

Diarmuid fell asleep again and again the voice of the hound woke him. When it happened the third time it was already dawn and he leaped from the bed, telling Grainne not to worry, that he would take his own hound along with him and his magic spear.

He set off up Ben Bulben and when he reached the top of the mountain, who did he see, sitting on a rock, but Fionn, alone and looking sleepy.

Diarmuid was suspicious at once. 'What's your game?' he asked. 'I know now that it must have been you mimicking a hound that got me up here. What are you going to do now—try to murder me?'

'Relax,' said Fionn, 'but not too much. That was a real hound you heard, for me and the rest of the lads have been out hunting the boar of Ben Bulben all night and the brute has already killed ten of my warriors and several dogs. That hound you heard was some poor animal being torn apart by those cruel tusks.

'So I'm off now and so should you be. That boar is too dangerous for any of us to confront. I know if you saw the size of it you'd be frightened out of your wits.'

'Are you trying to suggest that I am a coward?'

'There's no shame in being afraid of such a monster, especially for someone like you, retired from the Fianna, so to speak, and living a womanly sort of life for so long.'

Diarmuid was so furious he didn't even answer, but calling his hound to heel set off down the other side of Ben Bulben. Within seconds he heard a tearing through the undergrowth and a loud snorting sound. And suddenly he was face to face with a huge black boar. The creature had small red eyes that seemed to flash fire and enormous tusks like those of an elephant and it charged straight at Diarmuid.

'Go for him,' Diarmuid ordered his hound but the boar lowered its head and lifted the dog on one of its tusks and threw him over his shoulder.

Diarmuid stood his ground though his heart was panting and as the beast drew nearer he raised his sword and aimed for its neck. The sword struck the hairy skin and broke in two. Now Diarmuid leaped right over the boar and when he was behind it he grabbed its two back legs, one in either hand. The boar began a furious tussle, trying to shake off Diarmuid who held on as the creature began tearing down the mountain, wrenching its huge body back and forth. But finally it succeeded in freeing itself and Diarmuid fell backwards onto the ground. The boar turned and charged and its great left tusk tore right through Diarmuid's body, ripping it from shoulder to groin. But even as he lay there, his blood and intestines splattered on the mountain, Diarmuid raised his spear and struck the boar through the skull so that it fell down dead on the spot.

Soon, Fionn came upon the scene and stood looking down at the wounded man. 'Water,' whispered Diarmuid. 'Could you bring me some water from the stream over there?'

Fionn ran over to the stream, cupped his hands and filled them with water. But then as he approached Diarmuid a picture flashed in front of his eyes of the handsome young warrior riding off with his intended wife and he let the water slip through his fingers. Twice more this happened and the final time Oisín, who had now come upon them, shouted at his father and went to fetch the water himself. But by the time he reached Diarmuid, he was already dead.

When Grainne saw the body of her husband being carried back to the rath she threw herself on the ground, crying out loud that she too wanted to die this day. Then she got up and, raising her hands to the sky, she said, 'But I will live; I will live so that I can avenge the death of my darling.' And she stared straight at Fionn who was following the other Fianna in the funeral procession.

That night Fionn came to her to beg her forgiveness but she shouted at him and threw a wooden bucket at his head. Next day he returned and the next, each time so humble, so contrite, that finally Grainne began to calm down and listen and as she listened she began to think of what her life would be like now with no one to protect her and her sons not yet fully grown. One day, looking in a stream, she saw that she was no longer young and that afternoon when Fionn came to beg her forgiveness as usual she decided that though she would never love anyone as she had loved Diarmuid, she could do worse than accept Fionn who, whatever his faults (such as husband-killing), had continued to love her through all the years, even now when there was more grey than blonde in her hair.

So they were married, much to the disgust of the Fianna, and the strangest part is, that they lived very happily together until Fionn had lost all his hair and Grainne her teeth.

TRADITIONAL
TALES THAT
STILL LIVE ON

❖

IUBDÁAN, KING OF THE LEPRECHAUNS

❖

Iubdáan belched and pushed back his crown. 'That was a really fine dinner,' he said. 'And now I'm in the mood to listen to a song. Eisirt,' he called to his bard, 'I want you to compose a song telling of the glories of my kingdom—the bravery of its people, the strength of its army.

'It's good now and again for all of us to realize just what a wonderful race we are, how no other race can compare with us in deeds of valour.'

Eisirt groaned. It wasn't just now and again that the king demanded such entertainment but every single night after dinner. Eisirt felt that it was time he learned a few home truths. 'I'll sing no such song,' he said, 'because it's all a load of rubbish.'

'What?' The king jumped up. 'How dare you talk like that to me?'

'I'm sorry, Iubdáan, but it's time you knew that we are not the greatest race in the world and that if our army set out across the ocean they would come to a land of giants. One of those giants would wipe out our entire army by just raising a hand. He'd swat them like so many flies.'

131

Iubdáan laughed. 'A likely story,' he said.

'It's true.'

'And where do these giants live?' asked the king, scornfully.

'In a country called Ireland.'

'I don't believe you—you're making it up.'

'I'm not.'

Iubdáan thought for some moments. 'Then you better go there and bring me back proof of their existence or I'll have your head chopped off for your outrageous lies.'

'No problem,' said Eisirt. 'And I can tell you my head is quite secure.'

Eisirt set out on his journey in a boat no bigger than a matchbox. It was only when he was out on the waves that he began to realize how huge everything was in the world outside Faoilinn. If it wasn't for the magic properties of the boat he would never have survived the journey, as waves rose all about him, waves that were higher than the highest mountain back home. Eventually he landed on the northern coast of Ireland and as he chanted a spell the boat was turned into a little horse with dozens of jingling bells festooning its harness.

It was the music of these bells that alerted the guard at the palace of King Fergus Mac Leide. He came out of his sentry box to see where the music was coming from and he looked up and down everywhere until he finally saw the tiny creatures at his feet. He knelt down and saw that the horse was a noble looking little animal and that his rider was beautifully dressed and bore himself proudly. 'Well—what have we got here?' the guard asked.

'Stand back, please,' Eisirt demanded, 'or your great gale of a breath will blow both me and my horse back into the ocean.

Go and tell King Fergus that Eisirt, bard to King Iubdáan of Faoilinn is here to see him.'

So haughtily did he speak that the guard ran to do as he was told.

When the sentry delivered his message, King Fergus stared at him in disgust. 'Have you been drinking?' he asked.

'Please, your majesty, just come outside and you'll see that what I tell you is true.'

So the king and the whole court followed the guard out to where Eisirt was waiting. They all gathered round, astonished. 'Ah, will you look at the little fellow,' said one of the ladies, 'isn't he just so cute!'

'How dare you,' said Eisirt, highly insulted. 'Stand back, all of you—I didn't realize how enormous you Irish really are. Which of you is the king?'

'I am,' said Fergus, amused at the creature's bravery.

'Oh,' said Eisirt, staring up at him and pointing. 'Is that the mark of an Irish king I see on your neck then?' he asked.

Fergus blushed and put his hand up to cover the unhealed, ugly-looking wound on his neck. This wound was something that he was ashamed of and tried to hide by wearing special high collars. 'Wherever you come from you were never taught manners. Have you never heard that it is impolite to be pass-remarkable? I could have you put in the dungeons for less. But you're in luck—I'm in a good mood and I admire your spirit so I'm inviting you into my palace.'

Eisirt felt a sudden chill—these were huge creatures. Then he saw the king's seven-year-old royal nephew. Although he was very tall he was not as bad as the others. 'I'll go with him,' he said, pointing, 'I'll let him take me inside.'

'Hugh,' said King Fergus. 'Get down and help the little man.'

The boy knelt down and extended his hand, palm upwards, towards Eisirt, who hopped up and was carried inside standing erect and proud in the middle of the little boy's hand.

Eisirt spent ten days in Fergus's kingdom and was fussed over and petted by everyone there. The king's carpenter even made him a tiny bed and a special table and chair which were put on top of the king's table at mealtimes. But Eisirt knew that he had to return to Faoilinn because Iubdáan would be waiting there for him. Besides, he was feeling homesick.

He went to Fergus to tell him of his decision. 'And can I bring your nephew with me as proof to Iubdáan that giants like you really exist?'

'As long as you bring him back to me in one piece.'

'You have my word of honour on that,' Eisirt replied.

When the people of Faoilinn saw Eisirt walking up the road towards Iubdáan's castle, with the boy beside him, they ran away in fear and barricaded themselves inside their houses. They had never seen such a giant as Hugh, the seven-year-old child, who in Ireland was not even considered to be tall for his age.

Iubdáan's army wanted to flee too but being brave they stood guarding the way into the palace, standing shoulder to shoulder, raising their spears that were not the size of Hugh's little finger.

'Call Iubdáan out then, if you won't let us in,' Eisirt said. 'Tell him I've brought the proof that he wanted.'

When the king came out he stamped his little foot and burst into tears. 'Why do you bring such a giant to Faoilinn?'

he demanded. 'Are you trying to frighten me to death? You are a hopeless bard anyway and I haven't missed you one bit since you went away. In fact I'm thinking of having you replaced. Get out of my sight—you and that . . . that monster!' Iubdáan only said this because he felt he had been humiliated in front of all his people.

Eisirt was so annoyed by this uncalled-for attack that he immediately challenged Iubdáan. 'I put you under *geis*,' he said. 'You are to go to Ireland, you and Queen Bebh and eat King Fergus's porridge. And you can take this giant, as you call him, back with you, for the king will be worried about his little nephew. This is a seven-year-old child.'

'Pull the other one,' said Iubdáan rudely. 'If this is a child then I am a mouse.'

But when they were approaching the coast of Ireland, the king and queen began to tremble with fear. They could see huge creatures, three or four times the size of Hugh, walking on the shore and there were farmers in the fields making hay into stacks that were bigger than the biggest mountain in Faoilinn.

'Please,' Iubdáan said to Hugh, 'take us to the king's porridge and then we can go home. Everything is just too gigantic in this country—I can't cope with it at all.'

'I want to go home now,' Queen Bebh wailed. 'If I don't I think I'll have a nervous breakdown.'

Hugh took up Iubdáan in one hand and Bebh in the other and hurried up to his uncle's palace. Because he could tell how scared the little creatures were he took them straight into the kitchen where he knew that Fergus's breakfast tray would be waiting. The bowl of porridge stood steaming with a silver spoon already sitting in it.

'There you are,' said Hugh, setting the royal couple down at the table. 'The porridge is poured out ready for my uncle's breakfast. All you need do is taste a bit and you can be back in Faoilinn by this evening.'

Iubdáan swallowed. The bowl was the size of the biggest cauldron in the whole of Faoilinn. 'Right,' he said bravely. 'Give me a leg up.' He clambered up onto the edge of the bowl with Hugh's help. But the surface was slippery and he found himself sliding down into the porrodge.

'Ouch!' he screamed. 'I'm burnt, my bottom is on fire.'

Hugh looked round, grabbed the cream jug and began to pour it in on top of Iubdáan.

'Now you're drowning me,' cried Iubdáan. 'What sort of uncivilized creatures inhabit this country?'

At this point Fergus came rushing into the kitchen. 'Nephew,' he cried, putting his arms round Hugh, 'I heard your voice. Welcome home.'

'What about me, what about me?' came a voice from the porridge bowl. 'Don't kings in Ireland have any responsibility for visitors to their country? Get me out of here before I drown.'

Bebh, meanwhile, stood on the table unnoticed. She was weeping and trembling and sure that her husband was done for. If he ever escaped from that cauldron he would surely be held captive by the king of the giants. Gathering all her courage she slid down the leg of the table, ran out of the palace and down to the beach as quickly as her tiny legs would allow her to and set out for Faoilinn to tell Iubdáan's subjects what had become of their king.

Now, though the inhabitants of Faoilinn were small they had a great sense of their own dignity and great loyalty to their king. When they heard Bebh's story they decided at once that they would go to Ireland and rescue him.

'We need every able-bodied man,' Bebh said. 'You cannot imagine how big these Irish giants are.'

'But remember,' Eisirt answered her, 'though they are big we have great powers of magic and we will bring our druids with us and rescue the king by cleverness rather than brute strength.'

Back in Ireland Iubdáan was the cause of such amusement that nobody wanted him to go home. He was so self-important, puffing himself up to his tallest and demanding to be treated with respect. 'I am a king, a proper king,' he would squeak while everybody in the court fell around laughing.

'Would you like me to have a special crown made for you?' Fergus asked. 'Seeing that you seem to have left your own at home?'

Iubdáan nodded, sulkily, not too sure that he wasn't being made fun of.

But Fergus had a beautiful golden crown made for him, with chips of real emeralds and rubies set into it. The royal tailor made him a wolf-skin cloak, warm and elegant and fit for a king. Iubdáan was mollified but still wanted to go home. 'I have my kingdom to rule over,' he said. 'My subjects need me and you cannot keep me here against my will—it is kingnapping.'

One day the sentry on guard came running in to the king. 'There is an invasion coming up towards the palace,' he said. 'Thousands and thousands of little creatures just like Iubdáan are marching along chanting and shaking their fists in the air. They look very fierce and angry.' And the sentry burst out laughing.

The army of little people approached the palace chanting, 'Give us back our king.'

137

When Fergus came out Eisirt stepped forward and said, 'It is all my fault that the king is a prisoner here. Give him back to us now, Fergus, or we will use our magic against you.'

Fergus was annoyed by this. 'I will not give in to threats,' he said. 'I remember your bad manners, Eisirt, how passremarkable you are and I'm not one bit afraid of what you can do.'

The next morning every cow in Ireland was dry and there was not a drop of milk to be had.

Iubdáan was delighted. 'Now you see what they can do—let me go.'

Fergus shook his head. 'I will not be bullied, and certainly not by little creatures like you.'

The next day the water in every well and lake and river in Ireland had been turned green and smelled horribly of rotten eggs. Fergus raised his chin in determination and ordered everyone to put out buckets and jugs to collect any rain that might fall.

The following morning people were woken up by the sounds of donkeys braying and sheep bleating and cows mooing. When they went outside to see what was wrong they discovered that every blade of grass in every field had been turned into black slime. Fergus called his nobles to the palace and told them that he was sticking firm, no matter what magic was used against him.

Iubdáan could see that Fergus would not relent. 'I can get us all out of this mess,' he told the king, 'if you'll just let me send a letter to Eisirt.'

Fergus agreed to this and Iubdáan wrote his letter telling Eisirt that Fergus Mac Leide was too noble a king to be frightened into something. What Eisirt should do was try to be nice to him, offer him something in exchange for his prisoner. Why not try bribery?

Eisirt came to Fergus and offered to share some magic with him.

'So—what can you offer me?' Fergus asked.

'A spear that will be the equal of a hundred in battle.'

'Keep it.'

'A harp that plays the sweetest music though there is no harpist there to pluck the string.'

'I like to see the harpist's face, that gives me as much pleasure as the music.'

'A knife that cuts without being held.'

'For goodness' sake—do you think I'm a baby that needs to be amused?'

'A pair of shoes that will fit any feet and will allow the wearer to walk on water the same as if he were on dry land.'

Fergus showed interest for the first time. 'Have you really got shoes like that?' he asked.

'We certainly have.'

'Then give them to me and you can take Iubdáan home with you.'

The shoes were brought to Fergus—an ordinary-looking pair of brown brogues. They fitted him perfectly and he tried them out on the lake near the palace.

'Wow!' said Fergus, as he glided over the water. 'These really do work. Iubdáan is free to go.'

And after a great banquet held in their honour the little people sailed away from the land of giants, glad to be returning to Faoilinn where everything, including the people, was of a normal size.

THE KING WHO LOST HIS EARS

———— ❖ ————

When the Tuatha Dé Danann were finally defeated in battle and went to live underground, they made sure that they could return whenever they liked to the world of humans. They loved to play tricks on mortals, turning milk sour or stealing wind from a fire so that it suddenly went out. They never spent much time in the world of humans, just short visits, and then usually only around Samhain.

There was, however, one particular goddess called Aine who had a real weakness for mortal men. She was known among her own people for her beauty and also for her flirtatious ways and because she was the daughter of a great god they indulged her and didn't mind the fact that she was forever leaving her rath in Knockainey and turning herself into a human so that she could find a man to work her tricks on. It was all harmless fun as far as she was concerned but she never forgot who she was—the daughter of Manannán Mac Lir—and so she always demanded respect from a mere mortal.

There was a king of Munster called Oiliol who often went hunting around Lough Gur and the hills of Knockainey. This particular year the hunting was very good and so he found himself one evening still out when it was just beginning to get dark. When he looked around and saw the light fading he was suddenly afraid for he knew that it was the eve of Samhain when the *sidhe* are especially active and up to their mischief and in Knockainey he also knew that there were several fairy forts and raths.

'Let's head for home,' he said to his companion, a youth who attended him at all times. 'This is no place to be on Samhain's eve.'

The two of them spurred on their horses and the horses broke into a gallop but as they were passing a rowan tree Oiliol put up a hand and pulled up his horse. 'What's that sound?'

They listened and looked around them. The sound seemed to come from the heart of the rowan tree. It was the sweetest music either of them had ever heard. They got off their horses, though the youth was reluctant for he knew that a rowan is always associated with the *sidhe*. Oiliol, however, captivated by the music, walked in under the canopy of the tree and there, sitting on a high branch, was a tiny little man playing a sort of pipe.

When the little fellow saw them he jumped down out of the tree and away with him, running like a hare across fields until he came to the river Camog which he cleared with one leap, still playing his pipe as the other two huffed and puffed behind him. Without Oiliol noticing, it had grown quite dark but now, suddenly, the moon came out and lit up what looked like a smooth, green lawn, even though there was little grass around, for the month of October had been cold with heavy night frosts. The lawn ended in a bank and the bank was covered in primroses. By now Oiliol knew that he was in the presence of the *sidhe* but the sweetness of the music and the heavenly scent from the flowers led him on.

He had almost reached the bank when a voice said, 'Nice of you to pay me a visit, Oiliol.'

'Who's there?' Oiliol asked. 'How do you know my name?'

'I know more than that. I know that you are a powerful king with a great love of hunting and an even greater love of women.'

And there appeared in front of him, out of nowhere, a beautiful young woman with long, golden hair and white, white skin.

Oiliol gasped. It was true he had a weakness for the ladies but he had never seen any woman as beautiful as this. And her voice—it was sweeter even than the music played by the little man.

He knew that this was no mortal woman but he didn't care. He had to have a kiss from those red lips no matter what spell was cast on him.

He reached out his arms towards her.

'Ah-ah,' she said, stepping back. 'A king is not permitted to kiss a goddess.'

'Please.' Oiliol moved forward again, believing now that he would die of love if he didn't get a kiss.

She laughed and shook her golden hair.

'Even a little one.'

'Not even a peck on the cheek. You may admire me as much as you like, you may get down on the ground and adore me but you may not touch.' She raised a hand and pushed back her hair and Oiliol saw her lovely neck, as long and graceful as a swan's. This was too much for him and he made a grab at her and gathered her into his arms quite roughly and planted a wet, sloppy kiss on her red lips. Then he began to kiss all along her neck, turning the white skin red.

'Mine, mine,' he said. 'I have to have you, I'm mad about you—I'll never let you go.'

'You're mad all right to take such liberties with the daughter of Manannán Mac Lir.'

Suddenly he found himself lifted into the air. He didn't know how he got there but when he landed on the ground again he saw, lying on the grass in front of him, his two ears. They looked as if they had been ripped off his head and they were covered in blood.

'I told you not to touch, didn't I?' Aine asked. 'You wouldn't listen, though, and what good are ears to a man who won't listen?'

'Oh please,' pleaded the king, 'put my ears back on.'

'Never. And from this day you will be known as Oiliol Olom—Oiliol the bald ears.'

Aine disappeared as quickly as she had appeared and Oiliol had to be helped home by his attendant, where a healer was sent for. But all he could do was bandage up the wounds, for the ears were gone.

And from that night onwards the king hid himself away in his palace and never looked at another woman—mortal or *sídhe*.

KING FERGUS AND THE RIVER MONSTER

❖

When Fergus Mac Leide was a young prince, before he had become king, he had gone swimming one day in a lake high up in the mountains. Nobody ever swam in this lake for it was said that there was a monster who lived there who would destroy any creature that entered the water.

Fergus, out hunting all day, had been too hot to heed such a warning and he had dived in from a high rock. The water was icy cold but very refreshing. Fergus swam for a bit then turned on his back and started to float, looking up at the sun. It was a lovely summer's day.

Suddenly, the water began to heave though there didn't appear to be any wind. The monster who lived at the bottom of the lake had seen Fergus's shadow on the surface of the water and came soaring up now to see who dared swim in his lake. This monster was a cross between a river horse and a crocodile only ten times bigger than either. He had a scaly pointed snout and a huge scaly tail that thrashed around as he swam and it was this tail that was turning the waters of the lake into a churning whirlpool.

145

His snout broke the surface of the water and he reared upwards, staring around with eyes like balls of fire. When he saw Fergus he opened his mouth and roared. His breath, which smelled of decaying maggoty meat, reached Fergus across the lake and almost made him faint.

The monster roared again and began to swim towards the prince. He moved like fire, his great tail lashing around, his hundred pairs of flippers cutting through the water. Fergus kicked for the shore, swimming with a speed and strength that he didn't know he possessed. He kept as still as he could in the water, turning his head as little as possible, trying to glide rather than swim, knowing that this would increase his speed. Nevertheless the monster began to close in on him. Now the water was breaking in huge waves over Fergus's head and he could feel the heat of the monster's breath, smell its foul smell.

The shore was almost within reach. Fergus made a super-human effort and as he did so the monster flipped head over heels in the water and the great tail reached out to trap the prince. Fergus thought that he was finished as he felt a sharp whack on his neck where the tail made contact. But it was all right, he had made the shore. He grasped at a tree root and hauled himself on to dry land, safe at last.

When he got home his mother, the queen, said to him, 'Fergus, what on earth have you done to your neck?'

Fergus looked in the mirror and saw a deep livid wound which ran from above his jaw-bone right down to the base of his neck. It glistened purple and smelled really bad. The royal doctor cleaned the wound and gave him a herbal preparation to apply every night. 'It should be healed in a fortnight,' he said.

At the end of two weeks the only change in the wound was that the smell was getting worse.

Fergus went to doctors throughout Ireland. Each one gave him a different ointment and told him that it would be better in a fortnight. At the end of two months, Fergus knew that this was a blemish he would have to live with. From then onwards he had shirts made with special high collars that hid the wound and he had thousands of rose petals distilled and their oil turned into perfume which he sprinkled all over himself to try and disguise the smell.

It was very important to keep the wound a secret, for the people of Ulster would not want a king with such a blemish and this made Fergus's life difficult and every day he wished that he could somehow be avenged on the river monster. He had never even got married for the thought of having to tell his wife about his secret filled him with shame. And how could he expect any woman to come close to him with that awful smell? 'I'll die a bachelor,' he used to say to himself.

Until, that is, the day that Eisirt offered him the magic shoes.

Now he summoned all his nobles and warriors and told them that he was going up to the lake in the mountain to slay the monster.

Since the day that Fergus had received his wound five people had been eaten by the monster as well as countless animals that had come to the water's edge to drink.

'Don't go,' his nobles begged him.

'Let us go instead,' his warriors said.

But Fergus had the magic shoes.

A whole caravan climbed the steep path to the mountain

lake. The warriors were armed with shields and swords, just in case, and some of the nobles had their servants carry up boats, though they hoped that they wouldn't have to venture into the water. Fergus stood on the lake shore. He put on his armour and then his magic shoes. Then he drew his sword and walked steadily out onto the water.

He moved across the lake as if it were a field. Nothing happened until he had gone a hundred yards and then the water began to heave. Great waves rose in the air and broke over Fergus's head but he just walked on, his sword drawn. Suddenly the monster's great snout appeared. His eyes flashed fire and his roar resounded round the mountains like thunder. Monster and king, they moved towards each other.

Three times they closed in combat and three times drew apart. The heaving waters had grown red but the people on the shore didn't know whose blood had been spilled. Then the monster reared up, high as a mountain peak. There was a flash as Fergus raised his sword and then all disappeared into the churning water.

'He's finished, he's gone,' the cry went up from the shore. 'Our king has been destroyed by the river monster.' The water seemed to be boiling, with steam coming off it. Many thought what a horrible death and what an unworthy end for such a noble king.

Then, suddenly, Fergus surfaced once more. He came up out of the water and began to walk but he was bent over as if by some great weight, it seemed. Then he straightened and started to walk more quickly towards them. The water had grown calm and the watchers saw that Fergus was dragging behind him the bloody head of the monster. When he got to the shore, five warriors ran forward and beween them dragged the monster's head up onto dry land. Cheers of delight rose among the king's people, delight and pride that they had such a ruler.

Fergus smiled and began to undo his armour. The blood of the monster covered his upper body. 'I'll just clean this off,' he said, dunking himself in the lake. Then he stood up out of the water, spreading his arms, a happy smile on his face. There was not a blemish to be seen on any part of his body.

'I'll always be grateful to that little creature Eisirt for giving me the magic shoes,' Fergus said to himself. 'And now my next job will be to find myself a wife.'

Pronunciation Guide and Glossary

❖

Aillil: Al-yell

Aoife: Ee-fa

Bebh: Bev

Cian: Kee-an

Cathbad: Kuh-vhed

Cearnach: Kar-nuk

Conchubhar: Kon-who-hur

Cúchulainn: Koo-hull-inn (The name means Hound of Ulster)

Derravaragh: Der-a-va-ra

Eisirt: Esh-irt

Eithlinn: Eh-leen

Emhain Macha: Ow-an Mocka

Eochaidh: Uk-ee

Etáin: Eth-awn

Fiachra: Fee-ak-ra

Fionn: Fee-yunn

Fionnuala: Finn-noo-a-la

Fionn Mac Cumhaill: Fee-yunn Muk Koo-al

Fuamnach: Foo-am noch

Inishglora: Inn-ishglo-ra

Iubddán: Yub-a-dawn

Lebhorcham: Low-er hum

Lugh: Loo

Mac Leide: Mok Lay-deh

Manannán Mac Lir: Man-an-awn Mok Lir

Midir: Mid-ir

Naoise: Nee-sheh

Niamh: Nee-av

Nuada: Noo-ada

Oisín: Ush-een

Sadhbh: Sigh-av

Samhain: Sow-ann (Pagan Celtic festival, associated with magic; present day Hallowe'en)

Sceolan: Sce-o-lawn

Sídhe: Shee (The fairies, little people who live in forts underground)

Tír na nÓg: Teer nah nogue (The land of youth, where nobody grows old)

Tuatha Dé Danann: Too-ha Day Dann-ann (Very early inhabitants of the island of Ireland who, when they were defeated in battle, went undergound and became the *Sídhe*)

Uisneach: Ush-noch